DIALOGUE *with an* ANGEL

THE SPIRIT OF LOVE

FRIEDHELM HERMESMANN

Suite 300 – 990 Fort Street
Victoria, BC, Canada V8V 3K2
www.friesenpress.com

First Edition — 2014

ISBN
978-1-4602-5406-6 (Hardcover)
978-1-4602-5407-3 (Paperback)
978-1-4602-5408-0 (eBook)

1. Fiction, Christian

Distributed to the trade by The Ingram Book Company

PREFACE

WE ALL, BELIEVERS AND NON-BELIEVERS ALIKE, will be faced during our lifetime or at the point of death with the same fundamental question. This question relates to our relationship to God. While it is impossible for each of us to comprehend God and understand fully the mystery of God we can still establish this relationship with Him if we are simply more loving and caring people in our daily lives.

The great monotheistic religions (Judaism, Christianity and Islam), teach that God is an all-merciful and all-loving God and that He is a God who cares for humanity. It is, therefore, not too difficult to grasp the will of God to be a more loving person in our lives, thus reflecting God's spirit in our relationship with our fellow human beings.

Once we have understood this basic fundamental principle, our lives will change, our relationships with our fellow human beings will change and we can face the problems in our daily lives much more easily. Ultimately our lives can be happier.

This book is not intended to be a theological thesis. It is meant to be thought-provoking, covering difficult questions with the help of a story that reflects situations in our daily lives. It is intended to be a tool for meditation and prayer.

It is a story where questions that believers and non-believers alike wrestle with very often are discussed. The story is written to relate to the reader the fundamental message of God's love for all humanity. It is supposed to be a joy to read and the ending is a happy one.

HARRY AND BEATRICE, THEIR MARRIAGE WOUNDED

HARRY, A VERY SUCCESSFUL BUSINESSMAN LIVING in Vancouver, was ready to make one of the most important decisions of his life. Looking out of his office window on a beautiful, sunny day in early spring, he felt privileged to be able to experience the beauty of his chosen city, a place where mountains and ocean meet.

Vancouver is at its finest in late March or early April. On this particular day the sun shone in a cloudless sky. A gentle wind from the southwest brought fresh air from the ocean, blowing away any traces of air pollution. The snow-capped mountains, rising to a level of 5,500 feet from the ocean on the north side of the city, presented a magnificent postcard picture.

The rains in the winter and early spring convert to snow at higher levels. It is not unusual that the top of the surrounding mountains are covered with meter-deep snow while the city below is engulfed in the colors of its gardens, parks and trees. There is no other major city north of Vancouver. The mountains make this impossible.

Only one road travels north along the shores of Howe Sound, a fjord penetrating about 50 kilometers into the wilderness north of this city of almost two million people. The picturesque Sea to Sky Highway is very beautiful with its many curves and corners bordered by the ocean on the west side and by the mountains on the east side. The highway has its challenges, not because of traffic or its curves, but because of the ever-present possibility of fallen rocks or landslides. This road is magnificent in its setting. It leads to the Whistler and Blackcomb mountain resorts, two of the top ski resorts in the world. On a clear day on top of the Peak or Seventh Heaven chair lifts, skiers can simply rest a few minutes and stand in awe to take in more fully the view of the snow-covered mountains.

Harry loved Vancouver. This clear and sunny day alone justified his decision, made years ago, to move to the city he had fallen in love with. It was not a normal, average day in the life of Vancouver. It was one of those grandiose days that Harry referred to as 'the ultimate'. Such days gave him a feeling of invulnerability, reinforcing the arrogance in him that was common to those who see themselves as just a bit better than others.

Harry loved 'the ultimate'. He was a stock promoter and trader in shares who not only worked for the interest of his clients but also for his own benefit. People in his office thought him to be pompous, overbearing and self-promoting. He annoyed people with his constant boasting of how smart he was in his investment decisions.

Harry was obsessed with making money and the bull market of the last years had provided him with many opportunities to further his cause. Years ago he had seen a film about stock manipulations on Wall Street in which his hero had proclaimed that greed is good, that greed is the main driving force to create wealth. So whenever Harry made a killing in his stock manipulations, he justified his actions with the statement 'Greed Is Good'.

Harry had some spectacular successes for a few years. Luck was with him when he had made some risky stock trades, especially in a major gold mining swindle in 1997. In late 1996 when the stock was at its highest level, he had a feeling that he should get in on the frenzy, but instead of buying shares, he had sold a large number of them short. He purchased the shares he had sold at a fraction of the sales price when it was discovered that 'there was no gold in them thar hills'. What was termed as the largest gold find in the world turned out to be the biggest mining fiasco ever. The profit he earned on this deal was simply huge.

These and other windfalls gave him the feeling of being invincible. He did not squander his earnings but accumulated his money in tax haven accounts in the Caribbean Islands. Years of saving money tax-free allowed him the financial freedom he so longed for. But his success and foresight also gave him an arrogant 'know it all' attitude. This did nothing to increase his popularity with his fellow brokers, or anyone he came into contact with for that matter. Most people looked with envy at his successes and secretly wished his luck would change, but he did not give them this pleasure. He carried on winning, stopping only to complain about the taxes he had to pay, which of course he did not because the profits were sheltered in tax-free accounts. He had hired the best consultants and lawyers who advised him how to avoid paying taxes by transferring large amounts into offshore investments and how to perfect this strategy.

Harry felt on top of the world this beautiful spring morning. He had decided to accept an invitation to a party given to a select group of wealthy people in Whistler by a brokerage house promoting investments in the Caribbean Islands or other tax haven locations. He thought that it would be a good idea to have his eggs in more than one basket. This party was promoted with all the trimmings: free food, free lodging, free entertainment, female company if he so wished, a taste of the real good life, a party that was right in accordance with his status as a wealthy individual.

This invitation also came at the right time for him because it gave him the reason to escape the dullness and dreariness of his married life. He was happy to accept. Secretly he wanted to find out how he could divorce his wife Beatrice and hide his wealth, so that in case of a divorce he would not have to share the money he had earned with a wife he did not love anymore.

Harry and Beatrice had been married for fifteen years. They had met in Montreal where he had attended Loyola University. When they met she was a beautiful, shy woman. He was attracted to this shyness because it gave her an aura of being secret and distant, a distance that he, a brash, self-assured, know-it-all student of a Jesuit-influenced university, found interesting and alluring. They had met on a rainy evening at the Montreal airport in the early fall. Beatrice, while intrigued by Harry's energy, ego and desire to achieve, was initially hesitant to start a relationship with him. She wanted to pursue her own career as a teacher. Her wish was to teach young children, especially those with learning difficulties.

Beatrice felt that this would provide her with a sense of purpose in her life to do something good for someone who had less, especially someone who was not fully accepted in society. However these goals were compromised after she had married Harry because of her desire to make her marriage successful. She became his wife—eager to build a life together in mutual love and respect.

Now after fifteen years of marriage she realized that she had made a mistake. Her workaholic husband's desire to be successful in business at all costs had consumed him. He had little time for her. Beatrice's dreams of a life together with her husband were shattered.

Harry's feelings for Beatrice had also cooled. In the first years of their marriage they both were passionately in love. Their friends and relatives frequently congratulated them on how well they were matched. Harry because he had made such a wise choice in Beatrice, a beautiful and intelligent woman, and Beatrice because she had married a successful, self-assured businessman with a great future who would be able to provide her with an appropriate lifestyle.

Beatrice and Harry were married in Montreal but had moved to Vancouver two years later when it was apparent that better opportunities for success were on the West Coast. Besides they liked skiing and tennis. What better place to tend to these sporting activities than in Vancouver?

Harry and Beatrice had three children. The first two were twins born in Vancouver, a boy and a girl. They were very close to each other and seldom let anyone, especially their younger, slightly handicapped brother Charles interfere with their relationship. Charles, the third child, felt therefore like an outcast. He was eight years old and was neither accepted by the twins nor by his father, who had never wanted another child after the twins. In fact, he had asked Beatrice to get an abortion, but she had refused. After that their marriage turned into a battleground of wills and the atmosphere between both Beatrice and Harry had become more and more poisonous. The battles themselves weren't outwardly confrontational; no explosions of passionate statements, volatile arguments or abusive behavior. Rather, Harry kept up a steady flow of little insults and subtle derogatory remarks, against which Beatrice had little defense.

She wished to have the opportunity to have intelligent discussions about the problems in their marriage, but Harry would build a wall around himself to be buried in financial reports of companies that he wanted to invest in. He reminded Beatrice, almost daily, of the fact that she had a good life, that he provided her with money and that she should consider herself lucky to have such a good and wonderful husband as her provider.

He neglected to tell her that he had one or two affairs during the last three years and that he had slowly tried to develop a plan to terminate the marriage in the least costly way. He simply did not feel it justified to share the wealth he, through wise investment strategies, had accumulated in the last ten years.

Harry came from a Catholic family. Under the control of his rather strong-willed mother he had attended a Catholic school, learned his catechism and after twelve years of schooling graduated in order to attend Loyola University. He did not have a great passion for his faith; in fact he was riddled with doubts. After many discussions with his university professors, he eventually concluded that God did not exist and if he did, he must have been a loser. He had drifted into other religions but eventually wrote them off as more of the same. He especially criticized the hypocrisy attached to many religions and used these arguments as an excuse to focus his interests toward other affairs, especially towards the pursuit of making money. Money for him had the only true value, a value that he could touch, a value over which he had control, and a value that he did not want to share with anyone else.

Beatrice for her part did not realize this obsession initially. She was a beautiful, sensitive and guileless woman, influenced by the many things money could buy. Of course, Harry showered her with expensive gifts. The diamond ring for their engagement, for example, was a showpiece, admired by many. Years later she would regret this gullibility and she began to grow more and more bitter, especially when she was faced with the lack of real communication between them. She became irritated by the little day-to-day occurrences. She felt hat if those irritants were not dealt with openly and honestly, they could shake their marriage to its foundation.

For example, Harry would not share in the household chores and Beatrice would complain about that. He would use that complaint as an opportunity to get his point across, his point being that household chores were really women's work and therefore hers and not his. His function was to provide her with a good lifestyle. She should be really grateful for that. His standard phrase was that she should be more understanding about the difficult tasks he had to face day-in and day-out to make such a lifestyle possible.

These battles continued unabated. Sometimes each of them thought they had won a little skirmish, but that steady dose of daily poison made their lives miserable. Their son Charles could sense these tensions between his parents, but because he was unable to express his feelings well he suffered the most. He loved his parents in his own way. He tried to smile, to work hard on his homework and to impress his parents with elementary facts that he had learned in school, facts that came so hard for him but so easily for his more intelligent brother and sister.

The boy would get upset when the twins teased him by taking away his toys, especially his little teddy bear, the only real friend he thought he had. He would cry hysterically when they took it from him and tossed it to each other. He would run between them trying to catch it but couldn't because his brother and sister were too fast. It was not a happy life for Charles and his mother, who tried to protect him from the other children and from the impatience of his father.

Beatrice felt more and more helpless, especially when Harry often indicated that they would not have had all this trouble if she had only had consented to an abortion. Further, during the last few years, the word 'love' had disappeared from their day-to-day vocabulary. Instead the words, 'You should have done this and that,' or 'Why did you do this and that?' were the daily subjects of conversation Beatrice and Harry managed to come up with. While Beatrice tried to the best of her ability to salvage some kind of common ground, Harry was always evasive and immediately put a wall around himself. He felt that any attempt to break this wall was an attempt to enter his private life.

Harry, for his part, did not consider himself a bad person. He provided well for his family and was able to guarantee a good upper-middle class lifestyle that was necessary to maintain his status in the community where they lived. Harry was self-assured and self-appreciating. He frequently said to himself, 'I do so many things for my family, but I am not appreciated at home for what I do. And besides, Beatrice has not been able to adapt to the demands of the lifestyle a man of my status and wealth has. She lives in a mindset of fifteen years ago, when, yes, there was some kind of romantic love, a love long forgotten.'

All these and other thoughts were on Harry's mind when he set out on this beautiful spring day to visit his consultants and their entourage in Whistler. He was ready to live it up and make a final decision about the divorce as soon as he was back home the next morning.

Because Harry loved 'the ultimate' he naturally drove a car that is advertised as 'the ultimate driving experience' a potent new BMW sedan, an automobile commensurate with his high-flying status as a successful investor. Once at Whistler he would seal the future for both his wife and his riches. 'My life has been going pretty well to date,' mused Harry, as he slipped his car into overdrive, 'but it's just about to get a whole lot better.'

THE INCIDENT

EVERY TRAVELER WHO DRIVES ON THE Sea To Sky Highway will see many warning signs on the road that indicate the possibility that rocks may fall onto the road. Harry saw the signs but did not pay much attention to them. Listening to his favorite talk show on this late afternoon, he locked the car into cruise control at a little above the speed limit. The sun was shining from the west, barely above the mountain range on the west side of Howe Sound. He opened the sunroof on his car so that the wind and the fresh air tingled the top of his head. Harry was happy because he had finally made up his mind to end his marriage. He would probably come to a settlement that would allow Beatrice a reasonable lifestyle. Since he had most of his assets hidden from her, just as he had it hidden from the government, he felt safe and sound. He thought that he was a reasonable man, a man who, even though he did not love his wife anymore, could guarantee a good life for her and the children.

Deep in thought, he carried on driving. He was surprised that the traffic was relatively light. There were hardly any cars on the road, in fact only one that was traveling approximately one or two kilometers behind him. The traffic on the other side was also very light. He had not seen any car or truck on the southbound side of the road for quite a while. He was expecting to find a delay north due to maintenance or construction work.

He came around one of the corners and was confronted with an unusual sight, the sight of a motorcycle driver who obviously had no idea about how to drive a heavy motorbike. Not only was he driving way below the speed limit, but he was also driving the machine like a person who had never taken a lesson. He moved from one side to the other, jerking the engine up and then down, slowing it to 5 km/h and then speeding it up to more than 35 km/h.

'This is a sight unseen,' said Harry laughing to himself, 'Here is a Hell's Angel who doesn't know how to control a Harley Davidson. This has to be something new for these beer-bellied, tattooed bastards. This guy seems to have just graduated in learning how to drive a horse-drawn carriage, never mind a heavy motorcycle.'

After watching the driver in front of him for a short while and having slowed down his car to a near crawl, he finally became impatient. He said to himself. 'I have to pass this idiot! I can't drive behind this joker and wait until the next passing line. I have no time since I've got to be in Whistler in one hour. I am late already.'

With this in mind he closed the gap between him and the motorcycle driver who was still twisting and turning on the road ahead of him. The road was very narrow and the yellow double line indicated that the passing of any vehicle was forbidden and dangerous. Harry disobeyed these road signs and drove the car across the double yellow line in order to pass. While passing, the motorcycle driver made a final twist to the left side, almost hitting Harry's car. Harry was able to avoid the driver with a swift turn to the left, bringing the car completely into the southbound lane.

The motorcycle driver, upon realizing that a car was passing, immediately turned the machine toward the right hand of the road to avoid a serious accident. This meant, of course, that he would direct his motorbike toward the mountainside. Luckily, he was able to slow the machine down and turn it around back to the northbound lane. A possible disaster had been narrowly avoided.

Harry, in his impatience, was not so lucky. He was able to avoid hitting the motorcycle driver, but by putting all his attention onto the scene in front of him, he didn't see the upcoming sharp turn of the road to the right. At the last moment he swiftly steered the car to the right. He quickly looked in the mirror to try to see what had happened to the motorcycle driver, but that distracted him from seeing the football-sized rock in the northbound lane, which of course had sharp edges. Worse, it sat in the middle of the road bordering the double yellow line.

Like a magnet, Harry's car was drawn to the rock. The rock hit the inside of the front left tire of the car and the force of the speed with which Harry was driving resulted in a blowout. The best tires in the world, even the ones that were installed on his car advertised as 'the ultimate driving experience' could not withstand the force of a deep cut. Harry almost lost control of the car because of this force. He immediately reduced his speed and was lucky. If he had hit the rock at the speed of 80 km/h he would have lost control of his vehicle for certain. But at 40 km/h, he managed to maintain control and steer the car to a nearby lookout on the west side of the road.

Harry stumbled full of anger out of his car and had a closer look at the tire to see whether the damage was very serious or not. What he saw made him more furious. The first barrage of swearing was directed at the government, which, despite all the taxes being paid by its citizens, was unable to maintain a safe road. Of course, he overlooked the fact that he himself paid very few taxes. The next barrage was directed toward that stupid driver of the motorcycle. If this driver had only known how to drive his vehicle Harry would have been able to keep all his attention on the road. He surely would have then been able to avoid hitting the rock.

Harry opened the trunk to pick up the tools to change the tire. Suddenly he heard the roaring noise of a motorcycle. He looked up and saw the driver whom he had met on the road approaching him slowing down. He stopped and not knowing how to park his motorcycle leaned it against a nearby tree.

'Some Hell's Angel you are,' thought Harry, 'Not only do you not know how to drive a motorbike, you don't even know how to park it. I think I must have a serious talk with these guys and tell them that they definitely will have an image problem if they admit people who don't even understand the basics of operating a motorcycle.'

Harry also had another reaction—fear. Deep down he realized that he could have been responsible for a serious accident. He could have injured or even killed this man. He was prepared for a confrontation as he searched for a wrench that he could use to defend himself. He prepared himself for the worst.

The driver approached Harry from behind and stood very close to him while he was bent over searching in the trunk. "Howdy," said the driver, tipping his finger on his helmet. "Having a good day?"

The driver was a strong man, about two meters tall and 220 lbs. He appeared like a stereotypic Hell's Angel in his leather outfit. He had a beard that covered most of his face. He looked rather fearsome.

Harry was prepared for a fight. He had just found a wrench about three feet long. It was a weapon to be reckoned with. Even though he was quite nervous and unsure about himself, he felt that this wrench could be a tool to defend himself if necessary. He was a bit of a coward and abhorred fistfights, but like a rat when cornered, would not give up easily. Harry turned around to face his enemy. Standing there with the wrench in his right hand, he immediately started to argue with the driver.

"This was all your fault. You drive like a cowboy. You drive like you own the road. You have no regard for your fellow drivers, who at least have to pass a driving test. I bet you don't even have a drivers license!" exclaimed Harry.

The man replied, "Not so fast my friend. I prevented you from having a far more serious accident. I helped you to slow down. If you had come around the corner a few seconds sooner, the rock lying on the road would have fallen through the open space of your car's sunroof hitting you on your head. The least you could do is say thank you."

"How do you know this? Are you some kind of magician or fortune-teller?" asked Harry.

"No," replied the man. "I am your guardian angel. By special permission from God I was sent to Earth to have a word with you."

"What do you mean my guardian angel? As far as I am concerned, you are a Hell's Angel and I doubt that the devil employs guardian angels," exclaimed Harry.

"Why do you think I am a Hell's Angel? Just because I wear a leather jacket, have a beard and drive a Harley Davidson must I be a Hell's Angel? It is time that you correct your vision, because your vision may lead you to assumptions from which you draw the wrong conclusions. Not every driver of a Harley Davidson motorbike is always a Hell's Angel," said the angel dryly.

"But you're wearing a leather jacket, a status symbols of the Hell's Angels," answered Harry with a few doubts on his mind, his confidence shaken. "Even on your jacket you have imprinted the words Hell's Angels. I saw them while driving behind you on this road."

The angel replied, "Have a closer look! Yes, you can clearly see 'Angel' and yes, you can also see a capital 'H' with an 'e' following it. But it clearly says on the jacket 'Heaven's Angel.' You should get your vision checked, and that is the reason I was sent here—to correct your vision so that you can differentiate more clearly between what is important in your life and what is not."

"There is nothing wrong with my vision," replied Harry angrily. "I know very well what I should focus on in life. I am a very successful businessman, envied by many for my success. I don't have to improve my vision or understanding about what is important and what is not. For me, success is money and the more I have, the happier I am."

"You seemed to be quite sure about the value of your money," said the angel. "I am not. Money has no value in itself. It is simply a tool to transfer value from one person to another. It makes the exchange of goods and services easier. If you, therefore, at the end of your life, sit on a pot full of gold or have a big bank account, all that is absolutely useless to you, especially when it's hidden away in a few obscure bank accounts in the Caribbean Islands."

"How do you know that?" answered Harry suspiciously. "Are you sure that you're an angel and not from the tax department?"

'I better be more careful about what I say from now on,' thought Harry to himself. 'Somehow I have to get rid of this guy. He is definitely getting on my nerves.'

Harry said loudly. "Listen man, I have to get on with my trip. Because of your stupid behavior on the road, I have a flat tire that I now have to fix. I have no more time for idle talk about vision. I have an appointment in Whistler. It's very important that I be there on time. I suggest that you carry on in your travels and I also suggest that you work on your driving habits. Please visit a driving school when you have a spare moment. Someone there could teach you a few things about driving a motorcycle like a real Hell's Angel, not like a guy who has barely graduated to be in control of a horse-drawn carriage."

"Funny that you should say this," replied the angel. "I used to drive a chariot in my days as a soldier in the Roman army. I guess because of that expertise I was asked to try this Harley Davidson. Sorry I couldn't control this motorbike better. Even as an angel you never stop learning."

"But to prove that I am who I say I am," continued the angel, "I will fix your tire in no time at all. You see I can work miracles and where I come from time is of no essence. Time as you know it does not exist there."

Harry reluctantly put the wrench back into the trunk, and after a moment of silence the angel asked, "Do you have a watch?" Harry looked in astonishment at his watch and said. "Yes, of course, it is one of my Rolexes. I like to wear a different brand of expensive Swiss-made watches every day of the week. Today is Rolex day. In fact it is exactly 5:55 p.m."

Harry thought to himself, 'If this guy is for real, than I should give him a try and let him prove himself.' Out loud he continued. "You say you can fix this tire in no time flat? I believe that this tire, because of its deep cut, isn't even fixable. But I'll give you a chance to work a miracle. Prove to me that you are an angel and fix this tire in no time!"

"OK!" said the Angel. "But there is a condition attached to it."

"And what is that?"

"The condition is that we have a little chat about what is important in your life, so that your perception about what 'the real ultimate' is in your life can be improved."

"I have no time for long discussions. I want to get going and I need the tire fixed. You can fix the tire, but no long discussions about some spiritual stuff that I don't care about anyway," said Harry.

The angel replied. "I guarantee you personally that you will not lose any time with me when we have our discussion because we will be in a timeless environment. Therefore if you wish, you can carry on with your trip after our chat and you still can be on time with your tax consultants in Whistler. In fact I'll even save you time. Your tire can be fixed with a touch. You don't even have to remove the wheel."

"Well," said Harry reluctantly, "Let's get going then. You fix the tire and I will agree to a talk. But before I agree, I suggest you tell me a little bit more about yourself. Who are you really?"

"Thank-you, Harry," said the angel, "I will try to make my story as brief as possible."

THE ANGEL AND HIS STORY

THE ANGEL TOUCHED THE TIRE AS promised and both proceeded to a bench which was close by and sat down.

After they settled down the angel said. "As I told you before, during my life on Earth I was a Roman soldier. My name was Longinus. I was a common soldier in the Roman army. My father was also in the army and after retirement was allotted by the emperor a large plot of land in what is now southern Italy. My father was a good businessman and developed an interest in horse breeding. We bred horses for the army. When I became of age, I was conscripted into the army and assigned to ride horses or drive chariots when required."

The angel continued, "The chariot drivers were in big demand because the army required mobility in the occupied countries. Trouble spots were all over the place and one of the most volatile and troublesome area was the land of the Jews. As you can see, nothing has changed in two thousand years. The Jews were a stubborn lot and one of the most ruthless procurators was assigned to this part of the world to subdue the Jews. His name was Pontius Pilate."

"You mean Pontius Pilate, the man who judged Jesus?" asked Harry.

"Yes, the same Pontius Pilate," answered the angel. "In fact Pontius Pilate was my superior and I was present at the trial of Jesus. Would you like to hear about the proceedings of this trial?"

Harry said, "Yes. That would be interesting."

The angel said, "I was one of the soldiers who flogged Jesus, put a crown of thorns on his head and finally crucified him after a few hours of torment. I was also the one who ensured that he was dead by spearing him with my lance."

"So you are a witness of the crucifixion," exclaimed Harry. "That is very interesting. I always thought that the story of the crucifixion was an overblown event, touched up by two thousand years of Christian heritage with hardly any relevance to our present times."

Harry carried on, "You must know, I used to belong to the Roman Catholic Church, but I left because I couldn't attach any importance to the crucifixion of Jesus Christ. I always believed that the constant reminder of the crucifixion was to serve only one purpose, that is, to make the faithful feel guilty about the death of Jesus on the cross, which of course is a good tool to exercise control by the priests. It would be a good idea to hear from a witness who participated in the crucifixion. I would like to know what really happened."

"Do you want a vivid description of the crucifixion?" asked the angel.

"Yes, that would be great," said Harry. "Sometimes I still think about what the professors taught us at Loyola University. Therefore a description of the crucifixion from an eyewitness would really interest me."

"You will get your wish," answered the angel. "I will briefly describe the trial and execution of Jesus. We will use this description of the trial as the starting point of our dialogue, the real reason why we both have met."

The angel continued, "It was early in the morning on the day before the Passover feast where the Jewish people celebrate their freedom from Egyptian slavery. They commemorate on this day the events of fifteen hundred years prior when their ancestors were guided out of Egypt to the 'promised land' by their leader Moses. On this day Pontius Pilate was asked to judge a man called Jesus, a man whom the Jews said had proclaimed himself to be the Messiah, blaspheming God by making himself equal to God. Pontius Pilate was very reluctant to judge Jesus and hand him over to be crucified. So he first handed him over to us soldiers for a whipping and to have a little fun with him. He thought that this was punishment enough for a man who blasphemed a god about whom he knew very little."

"How did you flog Jesus?" asked Harry, full of interest.

"We hit Jesus with whips that had a piece of metal attached to the end," said the angel. "It was common practice in the Roman army to flog troublemakers this way. It was a very cruel punishment. Whenever you whipped a culprit, the metal piece on the end would cut a piece of flesh out of the body. The victim's body would be bloody in a short time, full of sores and of course weakened. We hit Jesus about twenty five times. This ensured that he would survive the blows."

"Jesus was strongly built, almost six feet tall," continued the angel after a brief moment of silence. "We whipped him very hard. Everyone had a turn. He was defenseless and, looking back, it gave us great pleasure to hit this defenseless human being. You know, when you are in power and in control and you are trained to exercise this power by all available means, pity does not come into play. The lust to see the blood of the unfortunate victim is the driving force. We flogged Jesus very hard and Jesus lost a lot of blood and physical strength."

"Is this the reason why Jesus was too weak and needed help to carry his cross to the place of execution?" asked Harry.

"Yes, that is possible," replied the angel. "Over and above the flogging we made a crown of thorns and stuck it on his head. This was my idea. I thought that this man was a revolutionary who had attacked the authority of the emperor by proclaiming a kingship based on an authority higher than his. I felt that a crown of thorns would be just the right thing to ridicule that kingship."

"When I placed that crown on the head of Jesus I pricked my finger. It hurt badly and out of anger I pushed the thorns even harder on his head. Jesus bled instantly. It must have been very painful but he stood there patiently and in silence. He looked me in the eyes, not accusingly, but more like a person who pitied me because of my lack of understanding of his mission and what he wanted to achieve."

"In fact," the angel carried on, "Jesus was not at all meek. He definitely never pleaded for mercy. He was more like a man with a mind full of determination to carry out at all costs a mission, the mission, as I understood it later, to prove that love is stronger than all the evil in the world."

The angel stopped for a moment and lowered his eyes in thoughtful silence. He then said, "I believe that Jesus was very much in control of the trial because he knew what would happen in advance. He went freely to Jerusalem and fulfilled the mission of his life, which was his sacrifice on the cross. Nothing could stop him on that."

"What happened after the whipping and the insults?" asked Harry.

The angel replied, "Pontius Pilate asked Jesus again where he came from and Jesus said that if he, Pontius Pilate, would know the truth, he would recognize his nature and what he stood for. But in his present mindset it would be impossible for him to comprehend the truth. Pontius Pilate was not used to this kind of language, especially not from someone whom he could, with a sign of his hand, condemn to death. Defensively, he asked 'What is Truth?' implying that truth does not exist."

The angel continued, "We will start our dialogue exactly where Pontius Pilate left off. We will start with the question of what is truth and how we can discover truth in our life."

"That would be a feat," Harry replied. "The only truth I know is the value of money."

"Well, we can discuss the value of money later," said the angel, not very pleased. "Let us carry on with my story. In order to continue, I have to tell you a little more about the crucifixion. We crucified three people that day, two murderers, some rough-looking characters, with Jesus in the middle. You must realize that crucifixion is one of the cruelest death penalties ever invented. It is a slow death. The suffering can last hours or even days. The Roman authorities devised this form of death penalty as an example of what would happen to those people who would challenge the authority of the Roman emperor and challenge the power of Rome itself. The victim is nailed on the cross. The nails are hammered through each wrist and through the feet. Not only is this very painful because the wrist is one of the main nerve centers in the body, but the victim suffocates very slowly. His lungs will collapse over a period of time."

"If this is the case," Harry asked, "then why do crucifixes in the churches and on paintings show that the nails were driven through the hands?"

"I guess," the angel answered, "years later the artists who created these paintings and the crucifixes did not have detailed knowledge about the methods used by the Romans. Remember, those artistic works were only created many years later, and what was written in the Bible about the crucifixion was used as the source material to create those works of art. If Jesus had been nailed to the cross with nails hammered through his hands, the hands would not have been strong enough to support his body hanging on the cross."

"In any case," the angel continued, "the body of Jesus was weakened by the flogging. He died after a few hours on the cross, while the murderers who were crucified at his side were still alive. We soldiers were asked to make sure that the victims were dead so that the bodies could be removed from the crosses. We broke all the bones of the murderers to make sure that they were dead. Jesus, because of his weakened condition, was dead already. I made sure of his death by piercing his side with my lance."

The angel carried on deep in thought, "Later on, after his resurrection, many people said that Jesus was not really dead, that he could not have been dead because he was only a few hours on the cross. I am a witness of his death, because I am the soldier who pierced him with my lance."

Harry asked, "How did Jesus appear to you at the most crucial hour at his trial and later on at his crucifixion? Was he meek? Was he defiant of the authorities? Was he revengeful to those who had delivered him to the Roman authorities?"

The angel replied, "I died as a Roman soldier a few years later, fighting the Jewish people at a time when Titus destroyed Jerusalem. I met Jesus as he really is, as the savior and redeemer of humanity. I talked to him about the events that led to his crucifixion and suddenly my eyes were opened. Suddenly I understood the reasons why all these events had to take place. I naturally felt very sorry about my participation in his crucifixion. But Jesus himself forgave me as he forgives everybody who does not understand the mystery of God and who is blinded by a wrong vision about what is true and what is not."

"You mean you met Jesus later in the next life?" Harry asked. "You have to be kidding me. I always thought that those people who killed Jesus were the first ones to go to Hell, if Hell exists. To me those soldiers who participated in the crucifixion had a free pass to Hell."

The angel answered, "Don't be too hasty in your judgment about what God should do and not do. Leave your human judgment and understanding of God's wisdom at home. It is time that you improve your vision about your faith in a God who thinks and acts as God and who is not a God whose actions have to be justified with human reasoning."

The face on the Shroud of Turin (believed to be the face of Jesus)

The angel continued, "When you see the face of Jesus as it is scorched on the 'Shroud of Turin', do you see the face of a revengeful man? Do you see the face of a loser? No, you see the face of a man, tired and overcome with pain, but also the face of a victorious man, serene, full of patience and love. It is a face that expresses the pride of having accomplished a great feat, a deed that is unique in the history of mankind. It is a face expressing compassion for his tormentors and in fact for all human beings, a face that proclaims to all humans the words: 'Father forgive them, they do not know what they do'."

Harry said thoughtfully, "I think we should have the discussion you wanted to have with me. I am quite interested in what else you have to say.

But be prepared for resistance. I'm not easily convinced to change what I believe to be true."

"I am prepared to do that," replied the angel. "We should make a short agreement."

"Good idea," said Harry.

THE AGREEMENT

THE VIEW TO THE WEST OF the lookout on the road to Whistler can be quite beautiful in early spring, especially on a clear evening. Anybody who has experienced the early sunset in spring with the sun appearing like a yellow ball of fire can be inspired to enjoy with awe the beauty of creation. It usually takes ten to fifteen minutes to see the sun go down behind the mountains of the Sunshine Coast to the west of the lookout. It was exactly this view that Harry and the angel experienced during the dialogue.

Harry, still doubtful but engulfed by the view of the sunset, said to the angel. "Please promise me that it won't take too much time for our talk and please fix my tire as soon as possible."

"Why don't you look?" answered the angel, "Do you see a flat tire?"

Harry turned around and sure enough he saw no evidence of the tear on the tire. Harry was impressed. He said. "You have a deal. Just give me a summary of what you want to talk about. But please no sentimental stuff where I have to fall on my knees. I haven't done this lately and I don't want to start with this practice any time soon."

The angel smiled and said to Harry, "You remind me of a dried-up cactus—dried up spiritually that is—a cactus that grows in a desert and longs for a little bit of water, a sign of life."

"What do you mean comparing me to a dried-up cactus?" asked Harry, angry at the comparison. "I find this insulting. I am a successful businessman, reasonably intelligent, trained by the Jesuits of Loyola University in Montreal to think logically. I have applied this way of thinking very successfully to my various business endeavors. Now you compare me to a dried-up desert cactus. This is a bit much!"

"I'm sorry if you think that I insulted you," answered the angel. "But I have to use a few hardy examples to get you back to basics. No, you do not have to be on your knees and no, you do not have to say your prayers. All I want from you is an open mind. Look at the sunset, how awe-inspiring this beautiful picture of mother nature is. All I want you to do is to sit here and quietly let this beautiful view sink into your mind and soul. Use it as a tool of meditation, a tool that we will need in our conversation. You must be prepared to develop the capacity to wonder, just like a child. It is easier to do this here than in a church, synagogue, mosque or temple. The wonders of nature cannot be surpassed by the best artists in the world. So I simply ask you to sit here quietly for a little while and take in this awe-inspiring sunset."

"You sure have a way with words," said Harry. "But I agree. Let's sit here for a few minutes and enjoy the sunset. You said earlier that in eternity time is of no essence. I can be convinced to think this way, and to prove that I can do it I will sit here in silence for a little while. But I will look at my Rolex occasionally just to see if you're right."

"Boy, you're a hard man to convince!" exclaimed the angel. "You don't believe me that I can make time stand still. Just be quiet for a moment and don't argue, otherwise the dried-up desert cactus will never be brought to life with a little bit of the water, called 'grace'."

Harry and the angel sat on the bench for a few moments enjoying the sunset. Harry took a deep breath and said, "You are so right. This is beautiful. You know, I often drive to Whistler but I never stop or slow down. I should really have taken more time to sit here and enjoy this miracle of nature."

Forgetting to look at his watch to see whether time really stood still, Harry continued, "Why don't you tell me now what you want to discuss."

"Very well," said the angel. "I want to discuss twelve topics which I consider important in your life and in the lives of a lot of other people. In the olden days, twelve was a magic number, a so-called code with which to explain a universal principle or multitude of people. For example St. John in his Revelations speaks about twelve times twelve thousand people serving and worshipping the 'lamb'. He meant an uncountable number of people. I am not saying that what we are going to talk about covers the total mystery of God and faith in Him. That would be impossible. But I chose twelve points for our discussion because I thought that it would cover a large spectrum of what is really important in the life of a person. I could have chosen many more, but I thought that the ones I selected are basic and you don't have to be a theologian to understand them. I tried to keep things simple."

Harry said impatiently, "What are the twelve points you want to talk about?"

The angel answered. "I want to start with my friend Pontius Pilate and explain what truth is. Then I want to discuss love because truth and love go hand in hand. I also want to discuss Jesus. Remember I went through a very significant change of heart, from one of his tormentors to one of his friends, an angel, who wants to relate that experience to others. Finally I would like to convince you, you whom I compared to 'a spiritually dried-up desert cactus', my apologies please, that you have the potential to become a very important partner in building the kingdom of God. You see, I will use a few analogies that you are familiar with in your business world. Finally I want to convince you that it is wise to do God's will."

"You make this sound quite interesting," said Harry. "You have fixed my tire. I guess I have to agree to participate in this dialogue of yours. I will try not to be too obnoxious."

Looking at his watch, which always was his normal routine when he made major decisions, Harry said full of determination, "Let's get to work!"

Both shook hands to seal the agreement and the angel, after a moment of silence, started with the first point of the discussion.

THE SPIRIT OF TRUTH

"HARRY," THE ANGEL SAID, "LET'S GO back to the trial of Jesus. During the trial Jesus said that he had come into the world to bear witness to the truth and Pontius Pilate countered doubtfully 'What is truth?' Do you know what is truth, Harry?"

Harry thought for a moment and was confused. He said to himself, 'If I answer money, the angel will say: money has really no value in itself because it is simply only a tool to transfer value from one person to somebody else. If I answer time, he will say: time in eternity does not exist. If I say the law, he will say: the law only reflects the guidelines of a system under which a community of people want to live. If I say this bench on which we sit, he will say: the bench is not made of solid stone, but of compressed energy as Albert Einstein proved in his theory of relativity. He will argue with me about what is truth until I am blue in my face. Maybe I should test the angel and tell him that I really do not know'.

Harry therefore said loudly to the angel, "My friend, I really don't know what truth is. Truth is in the eye of the beholder. In other words, what you understand under 'truth' is different from what I understand. Truth is a matter of vision."

"Right you are!" said the angel, "The spirit of truth does not come easy. It must be nurtured in your attitude toward things and developed over many years in your mind. Still it is the basis of any relationship you want to develop or maintain. You find the truth in yourself with proper vision. Like with a telescope, you must focus your mind on the truth. Remember the communist system in Russia?"

"Yes!" answered Harry.

"Remember the name of the communist party newspaper?"

"Yes I do. I believe the name was *Pravda*."

"Do you know what Pravda means?" asked the angel.

"No, but tell me."

"The name means 'truth.' The communist system was developed on a lie, the negation of the existence of God. The government named its main propaganda instrument, which was the newspaper *Pravda*, 'truth'. You see, truth is very hard to define, especially when you want to use truth to foster human ideas, political movements, philosophies and thoughts. Governments justify their actions because they believe they act and issue laws in the name of truth."

"There is only one real truth," the angel continued. "That is the truth which every human has to face eventually. That truth is God. Whether in this life or at the point of death, God will be the focal point for every human being."

"But nobody has ever seen God," said Harry angrily, "Nobody can prove that God really exists. You know that I myself wrestled with this problem for a long time. Yes, I was educated a Catholic. I even went to a university that is influenced by Jesuits. Now, after many years, I conclude that there is no God, that in fact God is dead. He has no meaning in my life. If God is the one promoted by the religious institutions, then I had better live true to my principles and remain an atheist or at best an agnostic."

"You remind me of a person I met once who said to me 'Thank God I am an atheist!' the angel answered. "Not only is such a statement absurd but it really is critical of the messengers, the organized religious institutions that struggle to explain who God is but cannot define Him in His completeness. Yes, God is a mystery. God is hidden. But God can be found with a sense of humility, wonder and awe, a sense that is so prevalent in a child. He cannot be found with intellect or human reasoning. God is unthinkable."

"St. Augustine thought precisely about this problem when he walked on a beach in Africa. There he saw a child. This child made a small hole in the sand and was trying to fill it with water by using a spoon. St. Augustine asked this child what he was doing. And the child answered, 'I am pouring all the oceans of the world into this little hole.' 'But that is impossible,' said St. Augustine, 'You must be out of your mind.' The child answered, 'It is easier to pour all the oceans of the world into this hole than it is to comprehend God.' God is beyond human thought. We only get a glimpse of Him through the one who came from God, Jesus the Christ."

"You use powerful words," countered Harry. "You can tell me all these things. I may believe them or not. But you still cannot prove that God exists. Why, for example, are there so many different religions in this world? If God existed, He would not allow this mess we have here on Earth. Most wars and now acts of terrorism, for example, are fought for religious reasons. Why would God, who is supposed to care for humanity, allow this to happen?"

"Good point, standard stuff brought forward by the average atheist," replied the angel. "It isn't God who instigates these wars. People start wars on the basis of what they think God should be. They want to superimpose their vision of God on others. But they don't know who God is in reality."

"Look, for example," the angel continued, "at these religions. Jews fought Moslems, Christians fought Jews and Moslems, Moslems fought Christians and Jews, Hindus fought Moslems and vice versa. They all pray to the same God in different ways. Each of these religions think that they have found the right approach to God. In reality it is their vision of who they think God should be, but not who God really is."

"Well, then who is God?" asked Harry impatiently.

"God is truth and unconditional love," said the angel, "As I said before, truth and love go hand in hand. When God appeared to Moses in a bush and Moses asked who he should say sent him, a voice—the voice of God—said, 'Tell them that Yahweh sent you.' Yahweh means 'I am' or 'I am with you all the time.' To be with you means that God is always there to care for you. You only have to realize this."

"This is interesting," Harry said. "Tell me more."

The angel answered, "Jesus, who came from God, gave us a glimpse of who God is in reality. He is the one who can testify with authority. The Jewish people found this preposterous and blasphemous. The Romans were spiritually not trained enough to understand what Jesus stood for. They thought Jesus to be revolutionary. Therefore when Jesus spoke of the truth, Pontius Pilate did not comprehend and simply put truth aside. He had no concept of the truth."

"I can see that," said Harry. "But how about our new scientific discoveries? So far none of the scientists have found God in their latest research."

The angel answered, "Scientists like Sir Isaac Newton, Albert Einstein and so many others discovered the basic laws by which the Universe exists. Yes, they have not found God in their discoveries. In fact for a long time, the Roman Catholic Church was very reluctant to endorse scientific developments because of fear and very narrow thinking. These scientific discoveries were hidden for a long period of time until the telescope was developed. With this instrument Galileo proved a new world system that Copernicus had developed. Until that time people believed that the Earth was the center of the solar system. It created a revolution of thought when it was discovered that this was not the case. You probably know that Galileo was called before the inquisition to revoke his findings. People were simply not prepared to accept what was discovered as true. They had a very narrow vision. Because of these and many other factors, people, especially the so-called intelligentsia, developed atheism as a theory. They could not combine faith with reason."

"But enough of all these sublime thought processes!" the angel continued, "I want to make you aware of another aspect of the truth."

"What is that?" asked Harry, "I thought there was only one truth."

"Yes, you are right," answered the angel, "But this is also a very important aspect of God's truth, namely that the truth lives in you as a spark of God's spirit. You are made in God's image because your soul is eternal. A spark of God's spirit lives in your soul, not only in yours but also in every other person's soul. This spark is like a grain. It can wither away and bring no fruit; it also can be fertilized—with God's grace, for example—to bring ample fruit. Whether or not the grain comes to full fruition, it still is embedded in every human soul."

"This is hard to comprehend," said Harry, "You mean that I have a spark of God's spirit in my soul? This is something I was not aware of and if you ask a lot of other people, they won't understand this either."

"Yes," said the angel, "God's spirit lives in your soul and in the soul of every other human being because the soul is created in the image of God. Therefore each human soul is destined to eternal life. All human beings have the capacity to love. God is love. So, if you love God or your neighbor, you bring God's spirit alive in yourself. That is a very important principle of any relationship, whether with God or with other human beings."

"You sure sound very convincing!" said Harry. "Tell me more. I never thought about God in the way you explained it. You mean the love I had for Beatrice years ago was a spark of God's spirit living in me?"

"Say it as you wish," answered the angel. "Love has many faces. I think we have to talk about love. We must understand what love is. Love is so hard to comprehend because we are influenced by so many other impressions surrounding us. But in order to understand God, we must reflect on love. Without understanding love based on truth we will not be able to comprehend God, if that is at all possible."

"Let's go back to your relationship with Beatrice and see whether you, in your own words, can define love."

THE SPIRIT OF LOVE

"HARRY," THE ANGEL ASKED, "WERE YOU ever in love with Beatrice? You don't have to answer if you don't want to."

Harry recalled how he had met Beatrice. It was on a rainy evening in Montreal in the early fall. The leaves were turning into the fall colors of yellow and red. It was relatively mild but crisp. He had just arrived at the Montreal Airport from a trip to the US where he had visited an uncle. He had been waiting for a taxi and so had Beatrice. Since he had been short of money, he had simply asked her whether she would like to share the cost of a taxi ride. He had been very flustered and apologetic about his request and for a short time his whole self-confidence was shot to pieces. This had never happened to him before. His self-assurance gone, he had wanted to open the taxi door, but could not because of being so nervous. The rain had been plastering down on his head and Beatrice had held her umbrella over him to keep him dry. Still, rain water had run down his neck, making him uncomfortably wet. He had said, 'I feel like a wet poodle' Beatrice had laughed at this comparison saying to him that this look would suit him quite well.

They had started a conversation and were still talking when the taxi delivered Harry to his destination. He had paid his share of the fare and left without asking for her name or asking whether they could meet again. At home that evening, he had thought a long time about this young lady whom he had just met and who had touched his heart. The more he thought the more he had the desire to meet her again. He had been so impressed by her simple elegance, the ease with which he could communicate with her, her innocence and openness.

'She is a natural beauty,' he thought. 'I must meet her again. But how?' He had looked out of the window into the rainy night and carried on, 'If she is interested in a relationship, then she might respond to a small ad which I will put in the local newspaper.' The next morning he had published an ad that read: 'Wet poodle, fully dry now, wants to continue the conversation with the lovely lady who came to the rescue last night at the airport.'

He had thought that there could only be one person who would understand this ad. He had never really expected a reply. But Beatrice had answered the ad. Thus a relationship had developed, culminating in marriage.

"Yes," was Harry's answer to the angel's question. "Yes, I was in love with Beatrice."

"What was your first impression of being in love?" asked the angel.

"My first impression was," answered Harry, "that love is beautiful, that it is an indescribable feeling of elation, energy and joy. Suddenly you find somebody with whom you can share your innermost thoughts."

"This is nicely spoken," said the angel, "but continue."

"I was in love," Harry continued, "because I found in Beatrice a person with whom I could communicate and share my true feelings. She was beautiful and I believe she still is. I was attracted to her sexually and spiritually. She made me feel like a real man. You must realize I came from a family where the word love was never spoken. My parents were busy making a living scraping by. It was hard in those days. They had a small business and their only desire was to make money and have a secure retirement. They never showed any affection to each other and lived side by side as strangers. In Beatrice, I found a woman with whom I could bare my soul. I could talk about things I never could talk about with my parents or friends. Beatrice gave me more security than she ever thought."

After a brief silence Harry said, "I pretended to be self-assured but I really wasn't. I pretended to know everything but I really didn't. My insecurity culminated in the pretense of being 'macho', showing off things, such as driving a fancy car, things that do not really matter. Beatrice saw through this farce. We sometimes had terrible arguments about what was important and what was not. I would never concede that I had lost an argument. I thought it was not 'man-like' to give in."

"Why do I tell you all these things?" Harry continued, " Is it so important to bare my soul in front of you, you who is a stranger to me?"

"Yes it is," answered the angel. "Please carry on."

Harry said, "Right now I am so confused that I ask myself the question why I ever married Beatrice. I don't know whether Beatrice ever loved me!"

"Never mind," said the angel, "you don't have to get sentimental. I am here for a reason. The reason is to make your marriage blossom again and, through faith and trust in God's love, help you to find what is really important in both of your lives."

"Harry, your first impression you had when you fell in love with Beatrice was that love is beautiful. You felt passion and desire for Beatrice; you felt joy when you saw her; you felt that you could not live without her."

Harry answered, "You said it, and I am sad to say that this feeling is gone."

"How did you express your love?" asked the angel.

Harry said, "Naturally we made passionate love, culminating in a wonderful, indescribable feeling of togetherness and unity. This desire for passion died after a few years because we became complacent. Love became a routine. The spark of passion was gone."

"It's interesting," said the angel, "that you describe your passion for Beatrice as unifying. God wants you to be one in spirit and flesh. Did you know that this is God's will?"

"I never thought about it," answered Harry. "It never occurred to me that God was interested in sex. At least that was the message I received when I went to church. Sex was never discussed; it was taboo. It was at best classified as an act for procreation, but not defined as an act of total self-giving and unity as we both experienced when we both made love."

The angel said. "What you say about passion and unity is wonderful. I see signs of life in you. Did you know that the greatest commandment that Jesus gave us is to love?"

"Yes," said Harry, "but I always thought that God's love was based on charity and sacrifice, never sex or passion!"

"You have the wrong impression of the love God wants!" said the angel. "God wants you to express the love he commands you to have as the love for your neighbor first and foremost. Your closest neighbor and best friend is your spouse. Love is the most important sign of unity between you and Beatrice and this act of unity can truly be passionate and pleasurable."

The angel continued, "But you can express your love to Beatrice also in other ways. You can express your love by sharing your thoughts, trust, friendliness, openness and acceptance. You can express your love daily by simply being your true self and helping Beatrice to be the best spouse you could ever have. Love is expressed in the little things in your daily life, not in great material gifts. They are sometimes just an excuse or cover-up for failure."

"As a true lover you want to make your marriage as successful as possible. That is hard work and commands commitment and humility from you and your spouse."

"You speak like a wise old man," Harry said. "It really isn't easy to have a happy marriage, especially when you discover after many years that your interests diverge. You said it rightly. It takes a lot of effort and commitment to have a happy marriage!"

The angel went on, "Harry, you were quite open with me with your thoughts on love. We must carry on in our discussion about God and Jesus. I used the example of your marriage to find out what you think love is all about. You sure have the capacity to love and to understand what God wants from you. We said earlier that if you want to find God then you must be able to love. Let's discuss in more detail the love of God manifested and made flesh in Jesus."

GOD, LOVE INFINITE

"I REALLY APPRECIATE HOW WELL YOU DESCRIBED the love you had once for Beatrice." the angel carried on. "You were very open with me and that is great. Your first impression was that this love was beautiful and fulfilling. It was based on trust and openness. You used the word unity quite often. Do you think that God's love can be compared to this love or do you feel that God's love is much different?"

Harry said, "I never thought of God in terms of love. In my early youth I thought of God as the creative power far removed from humanity. But at present I cannot concede that God exists. If I believe that God exists, then I cannot bring love and creative power into balance. One must come before the other."

"You see," Harry continued, "when I was in love I also felt vulnerable. How can you combine the idea that God is the creative power, a power which is unthinkable, with the vulnerability of a lover?"

"That is a good point," the angel answered. "Yes, God is the creative power of all that exists, but surpassing this creative power is His love. His love is stronger and more powerful than all the creation you can see or even imagine."

"These are mighty words you use," said Harry rather subdued. "You say that God's love surpasses even the marvels of the Universe?"

"Yes," said the angel, "otherwise His only begotten son, Jesus the Christ, would not have sacrificed his life freely for the redemption of all human beings. When God created the human soul, he gave it also the power to think and reason freely and the ability to accept or not to accept

God. With this creation He gave humans the ability to make a choice to love or not to love with the understanding that love is stronger than all the evils of the world. The sacrifice of Jesus on the cross is the proof that love is stronger than anything else."

"You see, before the Universe was created, God's love existed. The Universe is limited by time; God's love is eternal without borders or restricted by time. This means also that God's love is greater than what we see or not see, what we can imagine or not imagine."

"This is quite interesting," remarked Harry, rather subdued. "I really wasn't aware of the immensity of God's love, especially His love for all human beings. I always thought that the God in whom I had faith during my youth had forgotten humanity. That is one of the many reasons why I am a non-believer."

"I had my doubts that if God did exist, whether He had any power or had any interest in the fate of humanity, to prevent these wars, the poverty, acts of terrorism and inequality in the world. That is why I completely shut God out of my life and turned my attention to creating wealth for myself. At least I can touch it. God's love as you describe it, I cannot touch!"

The angel said, "I knew there was hope for you. You have the capacity to love, 'the real ultimate' in this life. The things you learned in your youth and even the happy memories of your early marriage are still on your mind. This is good news."

"But let's carry on with the faith that God's love is without borders. The Jews throughout their history had a close relationship with God, a relationship based on the law given by Moses. They sometimes saw in God a burden because He put them through trials, tribulations and exiles. Also their relationship was more distant. They would not pronounce or spell the word GOD. When Jesus taught that we could call God 'Father' they thought that this was blasphemy. Jesus was really the one who brought humanity and the faithful into a totally new, much fuller relationship with the all-powerful God. And this relationship is based on love."

Harry asked, "How did Jesus do this? Was this through the cross or through his teaching?"

"Both," answered the angel. "Jesus achieved this through the cross as the ultimate sacrifice and through his teaching to make people aware that there is a loving, caring God to whom we all can relate anytime through prayer."

His interest awakened, Harry asked. "How did Jesus tell his followers about the infinite love of God?"

"Mainly through his parables, but also through his example," the angel replied. "There are many parables that show the love of God. For example: the parable of the prodigal son. It should really be called the parable of the prodigal father, a father who is almost too wasteful with his love. The father is the one who unconditionally and spontaneously greets the son he thought was lost. The joy that the son, who squandered everything, came back is so immense that he immediately celebrates with his whole household. This is the 'gospel's gospel.' He is overflowed with joy when those who are lost come back. That is an example of boundless, unconditional love."

The angel continued, "There are other parables that show the unending love and patience of God the Father. Remember the parable of the fig tree. The owner of the tree wants to cut it down because it does not bring fruit. The gardener who represents God says to the owner, 'Let's wait a little while and fertilize the tree, with grace that is, and the tree will come back to life, bring fruit and so will be saved.' You see, once you understand more clearly the love God has for you, you will want to become a more loving person through God's grace. Every day will be joyful."

Harry was a now speechless, unusual for a brash, self-assured businessman who usually had answers for everything. His whole mind was in upheaval. He had never thought in terms of God's love in the way the angel expressed it so clearly. To him love was still more a sign of being vulnerable than being an absolute necessity to develop a relationship either with God or with his wife Beatrice. He was too self-centered to understand real love and it was not easy to overcome his doubts. But his defenses were weakened.

Harry said, "You sure can explain the parables very well even to non-believers. Is there any hope for me?"

The angel answered, "Of course there is, and not only for you, but for everyone else. Look at me; I was one of the people who crucified Christ and I am not in Hell. I am alive and well and live in the full vision of God, which is Heaven."

"But let me show you a few more examples of how God's love works. There is the parable about the vineyard owner who hires people to help him in the vineyard. The people who were hired last, just shortly before sundown, received the same reward as the people who worked the whole day. Human beings would call this unjust. But this is God's justice, which is based on love unending. There are so many other parables that reveal the love God has for the whole of humanity. I only want to describe a few because we want to cover other subjects too."

"To sum it up, Jesus came as the healer of the broken hearted and to forgive sins, not as the one to condemn humanity. Jesus the Christ, the one sent by God to Earth, came to reveal that God's love is unending, patient, not based on man's justice, and is unconditional. You yourself said that this kind of love can be beautiful."

"Then why did Jesus have to die on the cross when God's love is so well explained in the parables?" asked Harry. "I don't see the necessity of the sacrifice as proof that God loves humanity."

"Well," said the angel, "Jesus wanted to prove that he was capable of fulfilling the Father's wish and show the ultimate act of love, which is to die for all whom he loved. Jesus said clearly, 'There is no greater act of love than to give up your life for those whom you love.' Jesus loved all human beings, the sinners and the righteous, the believers and the non-believers, simply everyone."

The angel continued, "His sacrifice on the cross is the seal of approval of the new eternal covenant between God and mankind, the reconciliation between God and humanity, the redemption of all men and women. In order to prove this statement we must continue to discuss the person of Jesus the Christ in more detail,who he was and is. Remember though, what we discuss is all a matter of faith; it is not a matter of reason, and faith is the assurance that what we hope for is the truth."

"If you do not have the capacity to listen to these words with the mindset of a young child who experiences in the first years of its life fatherly or motherly love, in trust, wonder and awe you will never comprehend the fullness of the love God has for you."

JESUS, SON OF GOD, SON OF MAN

HARRY SAT ON THE BENCH IN silence for a while trying to understand what the angel had just explained. For him who had lived a self-centered life, God's love as it had been explained to him was incomprehensible. He had never loved selflessly, but only on the basis of 'What's in for me?' Yes, in the first years of their marriage he had been in love with Beatrice because he had found her very sensuous and attractive. For him who had been a little overweight and balding, to have such a beautiful wife was a status symbol. He had achieved the dreams he had early in his life: money, an attractive, intelligent and sensuous wife, and a family to be admired by neighbors. But unconditional love, as the angel had described God's love, did not exist for him.

While Harry sat in thoughtful silence, the angel started to talk again. "Harry," he said, "We must now discuss the person of Jesus the Christ in more detail. Who do you think Jesus was in reality?"

"Well," said Harry, "I know that Jesus is a historical person. I believe he was mentioned two or three times by various Jewish and Roman historians. Since they mentioned him and are a reliable source, I must assume he really did live and is not a figment of our imaginations."

The angel said, "Yes you are right. Jesus is mentioned by various historians. But we do not want to look at the historical Jesus. We want to look at Jesus the Christ as the center of faith. If we want to find out who Jesus the Christ really is, then we must put human reasoning away and look at him through the eyes of a believer. We must look at him for what he stood for and what he died for. We must look at him with a mindset in awe for God's plan of salvation."

"These words may be overwhelming. I hope that this discussion will not be too difficult for you to understand because I still see in you the doubting Thomas."

"Why don't you try me!" said Harry. "I have already had a few doubts about being a non-believer. I see already some new possibilities and maybe 'Harry the blind' will eventually get his eyes opened!"

Bursting out in laughter, the angel said, "I see you have a sense of humor, always a good sign of openness and willingness."

The angel continued, "Since the real nature of Jesus the Christ cannot be explained with human reasoning, we must approach Jesus the Christ with faith. I said before, faith is the assurance that what we hope for is true. In the gospels Jesus never said that he is God. Others, either the apostles or first believers called him Son of God. Many times saintly or holy people were called Sons of God. So, this expression is not unique to Jesus. However Jesus testified that he is one with God his father in spirit, that he is filled with God's spirit to the fullest and that he is the only one to know God fully. He is the truth and testifies to the truth. He spoke these powerful words with authority. Many people believed him."

After a brief moment the angel said, "One of the fundamentals of Christianity is the faith in the Trinity, God the creator, God the begotten son and God the spirit proceeding from both. To describe the mystery of the Trinity is impossible. But if you want to use human reasoning then you can say that true unconditional love finds its perfection in the love for another person. God's love finds its perfection in the love for His son through the Holy Spirit. By using human terminology and understanding we can compare the Trinity therefore to the fullness of perfect life, love and light. Aren't these wonderful descriptions?"

Harry said, "I guess this was very difficult for people to believe, that a man, a carpenter's son, a neighbor and family member, declared and taught that he was one with God in the Holy Trinity."

The angel said, "The faith in the mystery of the Holy Trinity was only developed over a period of time, many years after his crucifixion. It is too difficult to fully understand and beyond comprehension for the human mind. Therefore let us now talk about the human nature of Jesus the Christ. It is a matter of faith that Jesus the Christ has a divine and human nature."

"I guess it is much easier to relate to a real human being than to the mystery of how you describe the Trinity," said Harry. "How do you see Jesus in his human nature?"

The angel said, "Jesus is the focal point of all humanity, whether for believers or for non-believers, whether for saints or sinners, whether in this life or at the point of death. Jesus is the one who embraces all humanity in his nature. The expression Son of Man is an old biblical description of the one who will come to be the Messiah and the redeemer of humanity. Jesus uses this description for himself a few times in the gospel. His sacrifice on the cross includes all human beings past, present and future."

The angel continued, "Every human being has an eternal soul. The soul is God's creation. Being a human, male or female, is expressed foremost in the human soul, which is eternal and which is a spark of God's life, love and light in all."

Harry said, "You make it so easy to understand. If it is so easy then why is it that so many theologians doubt the nature of Jesus, doubt his mission, and see in him a spirit or a fiction or a religious fanatic. Look at the latest Jesus movement, a movement that analyses biblical texts. I understand this movement is sponsored by theologians, university teachers and other religious leaders. I remember that I had long discussions about this subject while I was still at university. They say that it is doubtful that a lot of what was written in the Bible about Jesus was not really spoken by him. They say that the only two authentic words spoken by him were 'Our Father'. The rest were insinuations or reflections."

"You are right," answered the angel. "The Bible has been demystified by many scholars and theologians. They are searching for the historical Jesus. You cannot dissect the teaching of Jesus like you dissect a dead carcass. Jesus as the Son of Man is embedded in the history of salvation as foretold by the prophets. We must see in Jesus the Messiah, the reason why the scriptures were written in the first place. He is the one who fulfilled the prophecies of the scriptures and the law of Moses."

"Then why did the Jews not believe and why do they not believe now?" asked Harry. "If you say that the Jews were the first people to receive the message of redemption of the human race, then why do they not believe?"

The angel said, "It is difficult to believe that Jesus has a divine and human nature and that he is the redeemer of humankind. It is a matter of faith, which requires a paradigm shift in thought. God is a mystery and the fullness of His truth will be revealed to everyone at the point of death when God reveals Himself to all. Then every human being, believer and non-believer, Jew, Christian and Moslem, Hindu and Buddhist, simply everyone has to accept Jesus Christ, Son of God and Son of Man as the redeemer of the human race."

Harry said, "I don't understand everything you have said. I never thought much about religion, especially not about theology. May I ask you a question?"

"By all means!" said the angel. "What would you like to know?"

"Why was it necessary that Jesus had to redeem the world through his sacrifice on the cross?"

The angel answered, "Let me explain this to you right now."

JESUS, VICTOR OVER EVIL

THE ANGEL ASKED HARRY, "DO YOU believe that Satan exists?"

Harry answered, "This is a funny question. Remember I have my doubts about whether God really exists. Now you are asking me if I believe that Satan exists. I can visualize that he exists because I see so many things wrong in this world. I guess there must be somebody who is a spoiler, somebody who disrupts, somebody who influences humanity to destroy, kill and hate. If God is a mystery, then so is evil."

"Yes, evil is also a mystery," said the angel. "Evil goes back to an event before the Universe was created. Evil is based on the defiance of the goodness of God. Evil is based on a lie. The Prince of Darkness, Satan or the devil—whatever name you want to use—has the ability to make a lie or untruth believable. Every aspect of evil is directed against God and also against the dignity of a human person. Should I explain this in more detail?"

"Yes, that would be great!" answered Harry. "I really have no concept of what you are talking about. To me this sounds very abstract. My understanding of evil was always that to have fun in life is evil, pleasure is evil, and maybe even greed is evil. I will be very interested in what you have to say about evil."

The angel said, "Let me go back in time, back before time existed, before the Universe was even created. Lucifer was one of the great angels serving God. He had a perfect vision of God. He, unlike all human beings, could fully comprehend God's life, love and light. He especially resented love. As a true lover you are giving something freely and unconditionally to somebody else. This also implies that you are vulnerable because the risk is that the one whom you love may not accept your love. Lucifer and his followers were not prepared to respond unconditionally to God's love. They were too self-centered and proud. They rebelled and were cast out of Heaven, which means from the light of God's vision into the eternal darkness. Lucifer, which really means the carrier of light, along with his followers were evicted from Heaven because of their pride and they will remain forever in darkness."

Harry asked, "How does Jesus relate to all that?"

The angel answered, "Lucifer still roams around like a 'prowling lion'. He, as the Prince of Darkness and as the father of lies or untruths, has the ability to present to humanity what is evil and bad as good, what are lies as truth, what is hate and greed as good and so on. Jesus the Christ came into this world to bear witness to the truth, what is really good, and what is really love. As the utmost testimony to God's truth, he gave his life on the cross, the ultimate sacrifice anybody can do."

"You see," the angel continued, "Jesus the Christ had complete faith in his mission, faith in the Father's will, the ultimate faith any human being can have. Jesus the Christ died on the cross in his humanity as a sacrifice for all human beings. He demonstrated the ability that even human beings can carry out the commandment of ultimate and unconditional love. The full realization of his divinity, his equality with God and his nature as the begotten Son of God, came at the point of his death and of course his resurrection from the dead. Through his sacrifice on the cross as a human being, a death freely chosen as the culmination of his mission on Earth, he destroyed evil and the result of evil, which is death."

Harry said, "It must have been hard for the devil to realize that a human, a being who is inferior to him, was victorious over him. That must have hurt his pride."

The angel replied, "Yes, but be wary of the devil especially because of his ability to make you believe that a lie is the truth. The devil, because of the ultimate sacrifice of Jesus on the cross, which resulted in his defeat, hates human beings. The devil wants to destroy humanity at all costs."

"You mean that this is the reason why we have so many wars, famines, earthquakes and the likes?" asked Harry.

"I doubt that earthquakes, famines and floods are the devil's work. Remember that the devil is a spirit just like God or the angels. The devil pollutes the minds of people, generations of people or even whole countries with untruths and lies. That process may take centuries. Remember time is of no essence in eternity."

Harry asked, "Do you have some examples that demonstrate your reasoning how evil exists in this world?"

"That is not to difficult to demonstrate," said the angel. "Since the devil hates humanity, every one of his acts is directed toward destroying humans. Let's look at a few cases that demonstrate the ability to make a lie to be believed as the truth."

"Let's look at slavery. Whether in Roman times or today, slavery is part of a culture where some human beings are considered a subclass that has no rights or dignity. They can be used as a chattel. They have no freedom and have to live in submission. If you believe that each human being is equal before God because of his or her eternal soul, which is a spark of God's living spirit, then slavery must be evil."

"Also Jews, Christians and Moslems are not free from evil acts even though they pray to the same God. For example the inquisition instituted by the Roman Catholic Church for centuries was an attack against human freedom and human dignity. The church tried to play God and judge like God. It justified political, earthly goals with what was assumed to be God's will. How can you argue with one who pretends to speak in the name of God? The only argument you have is to look at the result, the fruits of such a policy. The result was enormous sufferings by people who did not agree with the teaching of the church but did live according to what they thought was right. The act of condemning them was evil. It was an act against their dignity as a human person. Human justice was applied, not God's justice."

The Angel continued, "Only very recently, we have seen acts of hate and terrorism pollute the minds of people. Some people believe that they act in the name of God by using as basis a very narrow explanation of a law that they themselves created believing that this is the law of God. God is unconditional love. He cannot hate. Therefore it is the ultimate blasphemy to hate and carry out acts that are based on hate in the name of God."

"Also let's look at another event in recent years that definitely demonstrated the power of evil in this world. It is, of course, the Holocaust, an event where evil showed its ultimate power. The Holocaust was a result of ideas and actions developed over a long period of time. It was the culmination of evil that had evolved from generations of Christian thinking. When reading the descriptions of the event of the crucifixion, the reader may think the Jews were responsible for the death of Jesus the Christ. It was God's plan since the beginning of time to redeem humanity and destroy evil through this act of ultimate love. If at all, then the whole human race bears the fault. Over the years this wrong mindset created a relationship of non-acceptance by the gentiles. The Jews were always outcasts especially in Christian Europe."

"Nazism was based on the lie that Jews were a sub-class of people (Unter-Menschen), not equal to the German master race. They could be destroyed in the most efficient way without recourse to a consciously made moral and ethical evaluation. Through complete control of the media and infomation channels ordinary people were bombarded with this untruth day-in, day-out. It was an evil act, an act based on a lie, deemed to be good, but utterly bad."

"Do you want to know more about other evil acts that are propagated as good for humanity and are carried out as a so-called service to humanity, but which are based on a lie?" asked the angel.

"Just one more," said Harry. "I think I get the picture. I am quite interested in what you classify as evil in our day and time."

The angel answered, "A great evil which we face right now is abortion. The abortionists propagate abortion as a service to humanity. They kill and destroy the most defenseless and innocent human being, a flower of humanity that will never have a chance to bloom. Their act is based on an untruth, on a lie. Abortion is not only against the will and law of God but also against the dignity of humans who could have blossomed but cannot. God is the greatest defender of the human race, since he is its Creator. All His laws are given to protect the human race and human dignity. The untruth propagated by the abortionists is that the killing of the unborn fetus is deemed to be a service to humanity, and advertised as a good thing. A lie is made to be perceived as truth."

"I never thought about it in this way!" said Harry. "I myself contemplated abortion, but my wife Beatrice was against it. Come to think of it, that this was the start of our marriage falling apart. Interesting!"

The angel continued, "Harry, you are a businessman who understands value. What would you say if your most valuable resource that maintains your living standard and provides you with a future pension when you are old, is destroyed? Would you say that this is an act to be encouraged or discouraged?"

Harry said, "I would not encourage that because I like my comfort and I would like to have security in my old age."

"Well," said the angel, "abortion is not only the destruction of the most defenseless human beings. Abortion also kills those who might have provided you with a living standard you would want to have in your old age. If you kill the future of a country through abortion, then one way or another an economic price will have to be paid."

Harry said, "I think we have talked enough about evil. Let's carry on!"

"As you wish," said the angel. "As you can see human beings may not be aware of the evil they do to each other because they do not have the full vision of God's presence in their lives and do not understand God's will. Jesus the Christ is the victor over evil through his death on the cross. He also is the redeemer of the human race through his great love for humanity expressed in his desire to forgive sins. Let us talk about this now."

THE FORGIVENESS OF SINS THROUGH JESUS

THE ANGEL ASKED, "HARRY, DO YOU know what a sin is?"

Harry replied, "This has always been a subject that I have misunderstood. I really don't know what a sin is and I am sure that a lot of people do not understand sin either. The only thing I associate with sin is guilt and I hate guilt. So tell me what a sin is."

The angel said, "God gave ten commandments to Moses. These commandments are like a path on which to travel safely and in harmony. But what do these commandments achieve or what are they supposed to achieve, Harry?"

Harry answered, "I suppose if you follow the commandments, you please God and do the will of God. What bothers me, though, is that most of the commandments start with a negative, that is, 'you shall not.' It is a rather stern lecture and I can visualize a very authoritarian father waving a finger and saying, 'If you do this sin, I will remember it and will punish you for what you have done. This will teach you a lesson not to do it again."

The angel said, "Poor Harry! This is a complete misunderstanding of the Ten Commandments and what God wants from you. First of all, let me assure you that God is not an accountant who judges you on the basis of how many times you sinned. Second, God is not revengeful. If you think that way, then you still have not understood that God is unconditional love. If you are a lover, you don't count the failings of the one you love. If that would be the case, you would not be a lover. You would be a stern judge who would calculate all the penalties and make you suffer under these penalties as a just reward."

Harry said, "You say God is not just?"

"Of course God is just!" answered the angel. "But His justice is based on infinite mercy and love. You see, if you would have a full vision of God and fully understand the love God has for you, you would simply fulfill freely the commandments that God has given. But since your mind is inflicted and influenced by all the events surrounding you and your thinking is influenced by the way you were brought up, sins or failings are part of daily life."

"Then what is a sin?" asked Harry.

The angel answered, "You commit a sin if you fail to love and love means to help develop the best in your neighbor whoever that should be. Your neighbor could be your wife, your father, mother, your son, your daughter, a stranger, anybody you meet. If you love your neighbor fully, you would simply do what is best for him or her. But this love is incomplete in this world because of your lack of understanding God. So sin does exist. Sin is failing to carry out the commandment to love your neighbor and to love God."

Harry said, "How can I love God if I do not believe that God exists?"

The angel answered, "You can express your love to God in your love to your neighbor. Jesus classifies those people as hypocrites who say: 'Dear God I love you very much. I praise and thank you day-in, day-out, even on my knees in church for the great insight I have in loving you,' but then commit acts against their neighbors that are not based on love but based on greed, cruelty, hate, revenge, abuse, egotism, or whatever. To love is hard work. It is pleasant and pleasurable. Love is the source of happiness, but it demands discipline and commitment."

Harry said, "That is a very generic statement. You say that if I do not love my wife Beatrice then I commit a sin?"

"Yes, that is right!" said the angel. "We said before, that your closest neighbor is your wife. She is more than a neighbor ever will be. She is your best friend, your lover, the one who cares for you. It is God's commandment to love her to the best of your ability."

"What happens if she does not love me?" asked Harry. "What happens if we both decide to have a divorce? Is that also a sin?"

"It could be," answered the angel," because you also have a responsibility for your children who are dependent on you."

Harry said, "I don't want to go further into these discussions. These are my personal problems and one way or another I will settle them. I wish to carry on in our talk. You said that Jesus will forgive our sins, that we should have faith in his generosity and simply carry on in our way of life?"

"Don't be too fast saying this," said the angel. "Yes, you should have faith in the redeeming power of Jesus, but you also have to repent and have the intention of correcting your way of life"

"You see," the angel carried on, "God's love is so strong that He wants all human beings to share in His light, love and life. As atonement for the sins of all humanity, Jesus sacrificed himself freely on the cross. This act of love was so strong and victorious that it overcame death. Through this act of love, all human beings become destined to inherit Heaven, which is eternal vision of God. It is not only vision, but also God's sharing of His divinity with you in community with all humanity. I know this is hard to understand. We will discuss this point a little bit later. In the meantime I would like you to be assured of the redeeming power of the sacrifice of Jesus on the cross. Christ died for all human beings, past, present and future. So, as a beginning of your journey back to understand the love of God, you must have faith that Jesus will forgive your trespasses or sins, either in this life or the next."

Harry said," Forgiveness of sins makes me think about confession. I used to go to confession when I was younger and in all fairness I hated it. I was neither convinced that what I told the priest was a sin nor did I believe that I should tell my innermost thoughts to someone I hardly knew."

The angel said, "Your feelings or opinions toward a priest are not material in confessing your sins. To be a priest is a ministry, an office. The priest acts like an agent of God. Jesus delegated the power to forgive sins to his apostles, and they in turn delegated this authority to the ones who came after them. By confessing the wrongs you have done against the commandment of love and by your willingness to correct your way of life you will be reconciled with God. The spark of God's spirit, which lives in you, will grow and blossom."

Harry said, "You sure have a way with words! You must have been a romantic when you lived on this Earth."

"Could be," said the angel with a smile. "What I want to share with you is the evolution of my thinking from a soldier who was trained to kill and someone who never ever thought about the beauty of true love, to a lover through the grace of God. All people, even terrorists or people who hate have the capacity to evolve from a heartless soldier or profiteer to a lover who shares, from a taker to a giver, from a sinner who lives in darkness to a person who realizes that the spark of God's love lives in his or her soul. That is the redeeming power of Jesus. Is this not great?"

"Well," said Harry, "You have made me think about the beginning of my marriage when I was happy. I loved Beatrice. We didn't have much. What we had, we shared. We lived in the unity you bring up so often. Yes, those were happy times and sometimes I wish I could have them back."

The angel exclaimed, "Harry, I see a light at the end of the tunnel, literally speaking! There is hope for you as there is for everyone else. All you need to do is to reflect a little bit, search and acknowledge where you went wrong. It was probably not only you. It was probably the fault of both of you. The first step for a reconciliation is the acknowledgment of where you went wrong."

"You sound like a marriage counselor," said Harry rather jokingly. "But let's carry on in our discussion. I am finding our talk more and more interesting. In all fairness in the beginning, I didn't really take you seriously and I was afraid we would have a long, boring discussion about the existence of God and how that faith in God is transmitted through the ages by the religious institutions and churches."

"You seem to be so very critical of the religious institutions," said the angel. "They have a tough time just as much as everyone else in presenting the reality of God's spirit in our daily life. It is one thing to teach this reality. It is another thing to live it. The last part is so difficult. But as I said before, have faith in the redeeming power of Jesus. His sacrifice is the ultimate act of forgiveness. Jesus was not a coward. He did not abandon humanity to the power of evil. He gave us the ultimate gift, his life for all humanity. It is a mystery, an act that cannot be judged with human reasoning and understanding. It can only be judged through the eyes of God, and that remains to be a mystery or if you want to be more prosaic, His secret."

The angel continued, "We now have to discuss the fruits of the sacrifice of Jesus, which was his resurrection from the dead. As I told you, I was a witness of the resurrection, an unbelieving witness. Therefore I am impartial. Shall we talk about it now?"

"Yes," said Harry. "You won't believe it, but I am really looking forward to your thoughts on the resurrection. This sure is controversial. Be prepared, I am not going to be easily convinced!"

"Don't worry!" said the angel with a smile, "You might surprise yourself. You will realize suddenly that you, whom I called a spiritually dried-up desert cactus, will rejoice in the energy flowing from your faith in the risen Christ."

JESUS, RISEN FROM THE DEAD

THIS WAS AN EXHAUSTING DISCUSSION BOTH for the angel and Harry. They relaxed for a moment and were lost in their own thoughts. The sun had not moved at all. It was still sitting low over the mountains to the west of the lookout. Strangely, there was not a single sound from the highway going north to Whistler or traffic going south to Vancouver. Everything was quiet, the sound of silence, appreciated by so many but drowned out in the noise of daily life, a sound that invites people to meditation and prayer. Lost in his thoughts, Harry closed his eyes for a moment and a new feeling of energy and happiness came over him. He suddenly felt rejuvenated and joyful, a joy he had long forgotten.

He thought, 'The angel is right. A spark of God's spirit lives in my soul. This might actually be the wonderful energy, which believers call the love of God. Maybe there is hope for me, even so that I do resent being called a spiritually dried-up desert cactus! I will have to talk about this to the angel'

Out loud, Harry said to the angel, "You're a nice guy and I find you very interesting and what you say makes a lot of sense, but why did you call me a spiritually dried-up desert cactus? I am alive and well. I eat and drink well, and live a good live. I still resent this comment!"

The angel had expected this and he said with a smile. "As I told you before, you have a role to play in building the kingdom of God just as much as everyone else on this Earth. Yes, spiritually you were dried up; you had no concept of what this kingdom is all about. I was asked to help you to get your life back in order and help you to find out what is really important. Harry, you love 'the ultimate.' You demonstrate that in your daily life. You drive a car that promises to be 'the ultimate driving experience.' Your 'ultimate show-off' is to wear a different expensive watch for every day of the week. You have so much money that you want to find 'the ultimate' hiding place to keep it away from the government. You made 'the ultimate' killing in the stock market by selling short a couple of hundred thousand shares in a gold mine that proved to be a big swindle. But you have missed 'the one ultimate' that really matters and that surpasses everything you own or want to own!"

"And what is that?" asked Harry.

"Your faith in the risen Christ, Jesus the Christ risen from the dead and lifted into Heaven, thus opening up Heaven for all, even all the spiritually dried-up desert cacti of this world!"

"You see, the death of Jesus on the cross is, of course, the ultimate sacrifice, but his death would have been in vain if he had not risen from the dead. St. Paul says in one of his letters that if Jesus had not risen from the dead and, therefore destroyed death, our faith in him would have been null and void. The death of Jesus on the cross must be seen under the light of his resurrection. If Jesus had not resurrected from the dead, then the faith in him would have been a fraud. Therefore the reality of the faith in Jesus the Christ hinges, all in all, on his resurrection,the final act of victory over evil, the fruit of which is death."

Harry said rather reluctantly, "Well, let me tell you, there is so much controversy over the resurrection of Jesus. People just do not believe that such an act is possible. Further, they say that Jesus was not really dead, that he was taken still alive from the cross by his followers. They say that he lived for years in hiding and died as an old man. Even theologians doubt the story of the empty grave. They cannot comprehend the bodily resurrection. They say it must be seen as a spiritual event, very abstract, very unreal. What do you say to that, angel?"

The angel answered, "Just like many other miracles or acts of God, they are beyond human understanding and are a matter of faith." He continued. "You again have to look at the resurrection using as basis the Bible which manifests the history of salvation that started with the creation of the Universe but became apparent with the creation of human beings. All human beings have an eternal soul destined to be raised from the dead and live for eternity in the presence of God. Sin came into this world through Adam. It is not important whether Adam lived as the one described in the Bible or whether Adam is a symbol for the creation of the human soul by God. A human being is not as much distinguished by his or her body as by the eternal soul created by God."

"When God created human beings, He also gave humans the freedom to decide to be for or against God. God wanted to have a challenge. He sure found that challenge in human beings. God wanted to create the human race in his own image. That image is the eternal soul. He wanted humans to have the ability to freely decide between good and evil. He did not want to create a creature that, like a pre-programmed robot has no free will. He wanted to have a partner to overcome evil in this world. By creating the human race, he also made the promise that in the fullness of time a redeemer would be born who would lead all humanity to its place of destiny, which, of course, is Heaven."

Harry said, "I never have heard such a short format of the history of humanity before. Don't you think you are too abstract in your reasoning? It makes sense to me, but is not your statement too controversial and contrary to the teaching of the Christian, Jewish and Islamic religions?"

The angel answered, "The Bible was written thousands of years ago when there were only a few people who could read or write. The mysteries had to be explained in a language that everybody would understand. How can you teach these rather difficult events to people who had very little education, were mostly illiterate and had at best a very limited comprehension of God's plan of salvation? The best way to teach this truth is by simple examples, not through sublime trains of thought. I'm not privileged to know the full truth of how the human race was created. I can only tell you that the distinction of being a human is to have an eternal soul created in the image of God. I have said it many times before, that a spark of God's spirit lives in everyone."

"But let's go back to the resurrection of Jesus from the dead. You said that there are many, especially today, who doubt that this event happened, that it was impossible, that this event as described in the Bible ever took place. Let me tell you as an opener, there were many doubters right at the moment when it happened. The first doubters did not come from the ranks of the prosecutors but from the ranks of the apostles and the followers of Jesus."

Harry said, "That is true. When I read the story of the resurrection, the first thing I concluded was that the apostles did not believe, that they could not even imagine that such an event was possible and that they sounded very confused and were afraid. They were so confused that each of them reported the event differently and even contradictorily."

"Yes," said the angel. "The first non-believers were the apostles and followers of Jesus. They only were able to believe when their eyes were opened that this was the plan of God, that Jesus, in fulfillment of the scriptures, which document the history of salvation, had to die and rise again."

"How then do you really see the resurrection? Was it real? Was it spiritual? Was Jesus in fact dead or was he still alive when his body was taken from the cross?" asked Harry.

The angel answered, "Let me answer your third question first. Yes, Jesus was really dead. As I told you before, I ensured that he was dead by piercing him with my lance into his side. Thus, I can vouch for the death of Jesus. I wasn't there at his resurrection, but some of my fellow soldiers were asked to guard the grave, the entrance of which was secured by a heavy stone. This would ensure that the body of Jesus couldn't be stolen by his followers. The Jews were afraid they would do this and then testify that Jesus had risen. The funny thing is that the apostles did not believe in the resurrection either at first. Their eyes were closed just like everybody else's. How would they, who did not believe, steal the body of Jesus as proof that he had risen? A contradiction, don't you think?"

"Well, that may be," said Harry. "Still the doubt remains that there was no physical resurrection of Jesus, that it was a figment of the imagination, that we may have to see the resurrection in a more spiritual light, not in the light of reality."

"Harry," the angel said impatiently, "I thought we had made progress. You still doubt that the spirit is real, that the spirit is far removed from our daily lives. Let me tell you, the spirit is real, the spirit is the driving force and the energy of what we achieve in reality. Spirit and reality correlate. But to assert my point, yes, Jesus died as a human, but his spirit never did and descended to the dead to redeem all human beings of past generations. In other words his spirit never died, but Jesus rose also bodily from the dead."

"How could that happen?" asked Harry. "How could Jesus bodily rise from the dead and walk around, eat and drink and talk with his friends? This doesn't make any sense to me!"

"You are just like the doubting Thomas!" exclaimed the angel. "You just do not believe that everything is possible for God. Look at the latest discoveries in science. Albert Einstein proved in his theory of relativity that under certain circumstances energy, a force which has no mass, is changed into mass or a body which you can see and feel."

"Look at the other latest scientific discoveries, the effect of which cannot yet be fully understood. These discoveries are neutrinos. When you look at the stars, you assume that the stars, galaxies and black holes make up the largest body of mass in the Universe. This is apparently not the case. Neutrinos are probably the largest mass-components in the Universe. Neutrinos are the smallest particles ever discovered. Scientists speculated about them for many years in their scientific, theoretical models, but they had not been able to see or measure them, except very recently in scientific experiments in Northern Canada. These neutrinos have the capacity to go through all the bodily masses, like electrical waves go through the air. Electrical waves are energy, while neutrinos are mass".

"Why do I tell you these things? I only tell you this to make you aware that for God everything is possible, whether the creation of the Universe or the bodily resurrection of Jesus. The bodily resurrection of Jesus is simply a change from one bodily mass to another one from the physical body you can see and touch to the resurrected body in a different mass construct. I cannot explain all the secrets of God. I am not God. I am just an angel. All I am trying to tell you is, that the event of the bodily resurrection was real and that you have to have faith that this event happened."

Harry said, "It sounds plausible and real. Such explanations should give everyone hope, hope that there is life after death, hope that there is a powerful and loving God, hope that the life to come is a life of fulfillment and happiness!"

"This is well spoken. Congratulations, Harry!" exclaimed the angel. "You sure give me hope too that all these complex discussions are finally bearing fruit. Yes, you are very right. Jesus is the first born from the dead, a sign for all people that death is overcome, that death is really a transformation to a better life, a life in full vision of God, a life in full unity with God, a life in the loving light of God's presence."

"I believe that we should discuss this hope for a better life in more detail. I hope that you will see the potential for you and everyone else."

"That would be nice!" said Harry, smiling.

THE HOPE FOR LIFE ETERNAL

THE ANGEL SAID, "EVERYONE WANTS TO have a better live and everyone hopes to achieve it, non-believers and believers alike, simply everyone. Anybody without hope is desperate and at the end. To live without hope is to live in Hell, the eternal darkness. We really should discuss your, and everybody else's, desire to go to Heaven. Do you think it is a fair statement to say that everybody desires to be happy, fulfilled and at peace?"

"I think everybody strives to be happy and fulfilled. But it probably differs from person to person. My perception of happiness isn't some else's," answered Harry. "I have always thought and now I have my doubts that lots of money stashed away in the Caribbean Islands would make me happy. But I am changing my mind now that I have talked to you."

"I can assure you," said the angel, "that you will never find full happiness in this life and I can vouch for that statement. You will find your fulfillment when you live in Heaven in complete unity with Jesus the Christ, when you are engulfed in his eternal love, that can be compared to a ray of light of indescribable beauty. There is simply no better desire than to live in this light."

Harry said, "Can you describe Heaven? Can you describe your experience?"

The angel answered, "Heaven is difficult to describe because it is an experience that can't be expressed in human language. Your soul, as we said before, has imbedded in its core a spark of God's spirit. This spark may be dormant, very small or very bright. If it is very bright, then you are on the road to sainthood, if it is very small, then you have lots of room to grow into a saint and if it is dormant, then you are not aware that God's spirit lives in you and you wind up as a 'spiritually dried-up desert cactus'. Sorry for that description."

Harry said with a smile, "I forgive you. You see, I have learned a lot already. If you had called me a dried up cactus yesterday, I would have called my lawyers and sued you for libel."

"And now?" the angel jested.

"Now, I am learning to be a better cactus, maybe one with a few blossoms, a sign that even a cactus can be beautiful," answered Harry. They both smiled at this comparison.

The angel said, "We need to talk about Heaven a little more since it is life to the fullest."

"Please go on," Harry encouraged.

The angel carried on, "Heaven is a condition where you have life to your fullest potential, where you live in full community with God, where God shares freely His life, love and light with you, where you have no more desires but where you simply want to live forever. You are filled to the brim. You have reached your full potential."

"Is it difficult to get there?" asked Harry. "I still remember the part of the gospel in which Jesus tells his followers it is easier for a camel to go through the eye of a needle than for a rich man to get to Heaven. I am fairly rich, so where does that leave me? I am not willing to part with my money that easily." Harry paused only briefly before adding, "I also have another question. There is this gospel about the last judgment where Jesus divides humanity into goats and sheep. The sheep go to Heaven and the goats go to Hell. That's frightening. Are rich men goats? Does this also make me a goat?"

"Do not be afraid," answered the angel. "Remember that we discussed truth. Some people have a higher degree of knowledge of what is truth than others. The knowledge of truth is like a treasure for which you are responsible. If you are responsible for a lot of this treasure then God will ask you for a lot. If you have less knowledge of God's truth, then you will be asked for less. This treasure is the truth of God's spirit living in you and Jesus said clearly, 'The spirit blows where he will.'"

"You spoke wisely," said Harry. "But still you have not answered my second question. What happens to the goats? Will they really go to hell and how do you see the last judgment?"

The angel answered, "Let's talk about people, rather than sheep or goats. Yes, there are people, who after spending a life living in God's spirit on Earth, will go directly to Heaven. They come from all walks of life; they come from all corners of the world. Then there are others who will go to a condition called Purgatory. This is nothing to be afraid of. It is simply a period of adjustment and repentance that means a change of direction to prepare yourself to live in the loving embrace of God for all eternity. In other words you prepare yourself to be a more perfect lover. It is a condition where your vision is not impaired by the desires and disruptions on Earth, a condition where you suddenly realize the destination your soul will have to take to reach life to the fullest potential and capabilities."

"This is interesting!" Harry said. "To me Purgatory was always related to fire, pain and suffering. How about judgment? How does that work?"

"Well," said the angel, "you only really judge yourself. You see, in Purgatory you are faced with the full truth and with the full potential you had according to the gifts you had been given. If you did not measure up to what was expected of you, then you have to suffer. Suffering, not in the physical sense, but more in the sense of lost potential, which means what you could have achieved but did not or were not able to do. Your deeds have to be justifiable before God and if they are not, then you have to repent and change. I would say in Purgatory it is easier than on Earth. One thing you do not need, I assure you, is money!"

Harry said, "We talked about Heaven and Purgatory, but you never said anything about Hell. I always had the impression that more people go to Hell than to Heaven, that Hell is filled to the brim with lusty, fun-loving souls, while Heaven is only populated by a few saints who lived a good, but essentially boring, life of prayer. I always remember the statues of saints in my church who looked to heaven with such a holy expression that they appeared to be unrealistic."

The angel said, "These are only expressions of artists who wanted to capture the prayerful looks of a saint. I doubt very much that most of the saints were in constant prayer. They were people of real blood. Look at me! I was a soldier who ensured that Jesus died on the cross. I ridiculed Jesus and what am I today? I am an angel, thanks to the enormous grace of God. God even forgives the worst offenders. But let's talk about Hell. Hell is hard to describe. Hell is a condition of eternal restlessness, unhappiness and hopelessness. Remember that you judge yourself after having seen your full potential. Those who go to Hell want to go there. They also judge themselves but they believe in full vision of God that their judgment is better or more just than God's. In other words they cannot see themselves as a loving participant in the community of saints. They simply do not believe in love. They believe that God's judgment is wrong and the justification of their actions is right. I do not know whether this is possible because I have great faith in the infinite mercy of God. I also have great faith that God makes every effort to bring the lost soul back into His fold. Remember the parable of the shepherd looking for the lost sheep. This shepherd leaves all other sheep alone and searches under great effort for the one lost sheep until he finds it."

Harry asked, "Do you say now that Hell does not exist?"

The angel replied, "Hell exists and it is a condition of eternal damnation for Lucifer and his followers. They had a clear vision of who God really is and they rebelled. But I cannot see Hell to be populated with human beings. Christ's sacrifice on the cross and his subsequent resurrection from the dead was a victory over evil, a deed of such immense value that the whole human race was saved. Remember if you truly love, and everybody loves in his or her life, then you will live according to the plan of God, whether you are aware of it or not, then you are part of God's kingdom. God will not waste or forsake this spark of His spirit which He implanted into every soul."

Harry said, "I am impressed with your arguments. You told me before of the role I have to play. You told me that I had to change. Can you tell me now what you mean by that?"

"I will gladly!" answered the angel. "I am glad you softened your stance a little bit. You seem to be now better prepared for the great things I have in mind for you. What I expect from you is not really earth-shattering. But it is important. I want you to be a partner with Jesus in building the kingdom of God. How about that?"

Harry was shocked. He said, “Me? A dried-up desert cactus? A partner in building the kingdom of God? I am sure you can find a saint or some other holy man or woman to build God’s kingdom. Remember I have no experience in the spiritual aspect of life. I was spiritually dead as you so rightly implied. How can I build the kingdom of God and what does that mean anyway?”

“You’ll see,” answered the angel. “You’ll be surprised about the potential that you can develop in yourself!”

THE CALL TO BUILD THE KINGDOM OF GOD

"HARRY," THE ANGEL EXCLAIMED, "YOU ARE called to be a builder! You are called to help building the kingdom of God. This can bring a lot of joy into your life. Surprised?"

Harry was speechless. This did not happen too often to him. He always had an answer for everything and usually the last word in every discussion was his. He said, "My friend, you are kidding me. You call me strange names and compare me to a desert cactus, dried-up spiritually for years and here you tell me to build a kingdom. I don't even know what this means. What do you mean the kingdom of God?"

The angel answered with a smile, "I expected this comment from you. Shakes you up a little bit, doesn't it? Yes, I repeat, you are called to help in building the kingdom of God. Actually this is not too difficult at all. In fact, after we talk about it you will quickly realize how easy it is, and I guarantee it will be joyful. But you need to do it step by step because the kingdom of God is not a visible kingdom with a hierarchy and bureaucracy. It is a kingdom that you build within yourself, within your soul. Let me use an analogy. Let's assume you are an astronaut and you blast off into space. Everything in space is dark. You only can see light because it is reflected. The Earth, for example, can only be seen from outer space because it reflects the light of the sun. So it is also with God's spirit. God's spirit can be reflected in you through your way of life, through your loving relationship with your fellow human being, through the joy you bring to other people, through your laughter, through your positive energy. To do this, you must take the first step and this first step is prayer. Through prayer you invite God to be part of your life."

After a pause, the angel asked, "Do you know what prayer is, Harry?".

"I have not prayed for a long while," said Harry.

The angel said with an excited voice, "Harry, you really don't know what you have missed. Prayer is to communicate with God in a very direct way. Through prayer, you will experience the joy of God's friendship within you. God is not far away. God is very close and a spark of God's spirit lives in your soul. There are so many devotional prayers but the easiest way to pray is to simply to ask God to be present in your daily life."

Harry said, "You mean to invoke the spirit of God to be with me day-in, day-out? There are more than seven billion people on this Earth. Just imagine they all say the same prayer. God would have a lot of work to do to with them day-in and day-out!"

The angel said, "Compare God with being a source of light, a spiritual light that is brighter than the light of the sun. That light gives you the energy to sustain life as you see it. This light is the motivation to make you successful in your life. You just need to be aware that this is the power of God within you."

Harry said, "These are wonderful words you use. But you have to be more specific."

"Yes, I will," answered the angel. "Jesus taught us a very simple prayer which encompasses all that is necessary to pray. It is short, to the point, easy to understand and you can rest assured that if someone who comes from God tells you that this is the prayer you should use, then you can expect that it is effective."

Harry said, "You mean, of course, the prayer 'Our Father, who art in Heaven'. I have never thought very deeply about it. So why don't you explain it to me."

"Gladly," said the angel. "When you call God 'Our Father', you address Him as you would talk to your own father. Jesus wants you to address God like a child calling his dad. The Father is the provider, the listener, the one who cares, the one who wants to do the best for you. This father, whom you address in this 'ultimate' prayer, is the one who is present in your daily life. His name is holy, which means perfectly good in every way. In this prayer you petition the father to fulfill seven wishes. The first one is to ask Him to send His kingdom into your soul."

Harry said, "That is it? What do you mean by kingdom?"

The angel said, "Of course it is the kingdom of love. God's kingship is based on love and on nothing else. It is a gentle and kind love, it not a tough love based on threats and authority. It is simply a love offered to you freely like the father in the parable of the prodigal son offers it to the son who was lost and wants to come back. It means that you build the kingdom in yourself first and then bring the light of this love to your neighbor. You can do this in many ways: through kindness, through understanding, through smiles, through happiness, through caring, by simply being positive. There are countless ways to express love!"

The angel carried on, "The next petition is that God's will be done in building this kingdom here on Earth, where you still have the imperfect vision of God, in the same way as God's will is being done in Heaven, where there is the perfect vision of God."

The angel continued, "Then we ask God to provide us with the necessities of life. The next petition is to ask God to forgive our failings, which He does. In return, He asks us to forgive our neighbors, who failed against us."

Harry interrupted, "We come now to the next petition, where I always had difficulties. It is the part where we ask God not to lead us into temptations. How can God be a loving God if He is so devious as to lead us into temptations, in other words lead us to the possibility of failings? How do you explain this?"

The angel answered, "This part has been misunderstood for generations. God does not lead anybody into situations where he or she can be tempted to fail the command of love. In God there is no deceit. This part means that we ask God not to put us to a test. It is our lack of understanding God's will and our weakness, which may lead us to fail the test. Lucifer was put to a test and even so he lived in the full vision of God, he failed this test. You know what happened to him. In this part of the prayer, we simply ask God not to test us because of the risk of failure since we do not have a clear understanding of God's will."

"I never thought about it that way," said Harry. "Your explanation makes sense."

The angel continued, "The final petition is like a cry for help. Evil is in this world. Evil is sometimes not recognized. We have seen that evil is not fully understood by the human mind despite the progress made in understanding, who is God is and what human dignity is all about. Still the Father of Lies, the Prince of Darkness, is able to be destructive to the human race. He can inflict the human mind with hate, deceit and abuse in the name of God. Thus he can give the impression that to do evil acts in God's name is good. Such acts are the 'ultimate' blasphemy. God is unconditional love. He cannot hate or be deceitful."

"This is well spoken," said Harry. He continued, "I just had an idea that may surprise you. I believe that this prayer, in the way you explained it, is so universal and generic that it should appeal to all major religious denominations in this world, Judaism, Christianity, Islam, Hinduism and Buddhism. Just imagine if the Palestinians and Jews who fight over the right to live in Jerusalem would use this prayer every day. I could visualize a place to be built in Jerusalem where both pray together for peace using this and other prayers. They would be united in spirit and suddenly experience this unity and peace in their daily lives. Then they would really fulfill the will of God. Would it not be great to have Jerusalem become a city as God intended it to be, a city of peace and love, a city dedicated to the visible kingdom of God in this world for all humanity to see? It could be a city where everyone, especially Jews, Muslims and Christians can experience the love of God in unity. I doubt that this will ever happen."

"Harry, that is a wonderful idea," said the angel full of admiration. "You sure surprised me. You have made more progress than I thought possible. Yes, the rift between both the Jews and Palestinians is great. They both hate and do not trust each other despite the fact that they pray to the same God. God would love to see Jerusalem become a city of peace dedicated to the whole human race, a true symbol of God's kingdom. It can be done, but it requires love, tolerance, compromise and understanding. It requires that both Jews and Palestinians pray together in unity. The prayer Jesus taught is so universal, that it may appeal to both. This may happen in one of these days, maybe not in your lifetime, but for sure in God's lifetime. Remember God is patient. God as revealed through Jesus is the God of love and peace. This love will overcome the evil of hate, war and injustice and even will bring Jews and Palestinians together, so that they can also live in peace and harmony."

Harry said, "I am glad, that I surprised you. You see, I am willing to listen. In fact I find our talk more and more interesting. You sure have given me a lot of insight into the basics of building a relationship with God. Is this all, or are there other ways and means to build the kingdom?"

"Yes there are," answered the angel. "You can enhance the kingdom of God very much by celebrating the Eucharist."

Harry said, "I have not been to mass for so many years. I strayed away because I did not see any meaning in this ceremony. I was bored and I did not understand."

"That is too bad. You do not know what you have missed!" exclaimed the angel. "The Eucharist is where Jesus Christ makes his sacrifice on the cross present everyday in the form of bread and wine to the participants in a bloodless and spiritual way. This is, of course, a matter of faith, faith meaning the assurance that what you hope for is the truth. The understanding of what the Eucharist means and who has the authority to celebrate it is a stumbling block to the unity of the various Christian denominations. Some say it is simply a meal. Others believe it signifies the body and blood of Christ, but nothing more. The Roman Catholic Church teaches that the priest through his ministry changes bread and wine into the real body and blood of Christ. This is a matter of faith, but it is central to the Roman Catholic Church. It is the faith built on the teachings of the apostles, the first witnesses and participants of the first Eucharist the day before the crucifixion."

Harry said, "I guess the opinions about the Eucharist diverge quite a bit?"

"Yes, that is true," said the angel. "But if you have faith in God and believe that this is the faith of the apostles, the direct witnesses, then you should also believe that the Eucharist is the body and blood of Christ in His spirit. By participating in the Eucharist, you help to make present the sacrifice of Christ on the cross in a spiritual way. This act is the ultimate act of love and it is the redemption of the human race. You, Harry, by participating in this spirit in the Eucharist will become a partner, a junior partner that is, with Christ in the building of God's kingdom."

"What you say is overwhelming and I surely cannot totally comprehend what you said. In fact, most people participating in the Eucharist cannot comprehend this in its totality either," said Harry.

After a moment of silence, Harry continued, "You mean, if I participate in the Eucharist with the faith you just described I can help in the redemption of humanity? In other words I can help realize the kingdom of God not only in myself but also in others who are non-believers? That is incomprehensible!"

The angel answered, "Harry, you man of little faith! If you had the faith the size of a mustard seed, you would be an important partner in God's plan for building His kingdom. The Eucharist is Jesus in midst of the believers. Jesus is here ready to make his sacrifice present again and again in the spirit. Jesus shares His divinity with you and lives within you."

Harry was shocked. "I cannot comprehend this. Give me some time. Remember you compared me to a 'spiritually dried-up desert cactus'. It will take a while to bring this cactus back to life! "

"I will be patient," said the angel, "and I can wait. Remember in eternity time is of no essence."

The angel continued, "I would like to make you aware of another point that you as a believer should realize. This is the joy and trust in experiencing the friendship of God. Let us talk about this now."

THE JOY AND TRUST TO LIVE IN THE FRIENDSHIP OF GOD

THE ANGEL SAID, "HARRY, JESUS ASKS you to call him a friend. By doing so he implies that you also can call God a friend. Your relationship to God will be like a relationship between friends, not like the one between a master and a servant or slave. A friend listens, a friend cares, a friend shares. A friend is someone who will help. It is a real personal relationship available to you if you so wish to take advantage of it. Do you realize this?"

"Yes," said Harry. "I still remember the lectures from my olden days as a pupil in religious studies. We were taught that if you ask God for something you want, he will give it to you. All you have to have is faith. I remember many times I prayed for some favors, but I never received what I asked for. That makes it hard to have faith in such promises."

The angel said, "I am sure you are not the only one. Many faithful believe that their prayers never were answered. But they never gave God a chance to act or they expected something different than what they received."

The angel continued, "You must believe in providence, that means that God will care for you and provide you with those things that are really important in His plan. These are not necessarily those things that are important in your plans. Both plans may differ; however, in all fairness, God's plan has precedence over your plan. So it's quite possible that you never received what you wanted. But let me tell you something: you sure received what you needed, and much more."

"What do mean by that?" asked Harry.

The angel answered, "Did you not have a good life? Did you not find the love of your life? Did you not meet me, an angel? Here's the truth. You need me more than those tax lawyers and accountants who want to help you hide your money in the Caribbean Islands. You need to wake up and find out where you truly belong to, namely to your family. Beatrice needs you and so does your son Charles. You have to fulfill God's plan relative to your responsibilities toward your family. This is not an onerous plan, but a plan that will bring you true happiness, the happiness from years ago when you first met Beatrice, the happiness you had in your first few years of your marriage when you both were so young and full of hope and love. That is what God as a true friend wants you to come back to. This is God's plan."

Harry said astonished, "I never knew that the almighty God, the God of the Universe, the creator of all that is seen and unseen, has taken such an interest in me. After all, I am one human being out of seven billion people on this Earth and here I am talking to one of His angels who tells me that my prayers have been answered. By the way, I have not prayed for the last few years. I have not even believed that there is a God who takes a personal interest in my affairs. How do explain that?"

The angel said with a smile, "These were not your prayers, but these were the prayers of Beatrice and especially the prayer of your son Charles. You know that he has a few difficulties. He is not as perfect as you want him to be. You know that he may not be as smart as your other children. But God does not look at these things. God compares him to a flower that has not blossomed yet. But Charles has an unconditional faith and trust in God. Charles, even though he can't express his innermost thoughts the way you can do, prayed with such honesty, faith and trust that God had no choice but to send me, an angel, to have a few words with you. You see, prayers are answered. They may not be your prayers, but prayers from someone who loves you."

Harry was really shocked now. He had never taken Charles seriously and had often treated him like a burden. Charles was for him a continuous source of arguments with Beatrice, to the point where on one occasion he said loudly to his wife in front of Charles that he never wanted Charles in the first place and that an abortion should have been the right solution. He did not realize that Charles had understood what he had said.

Harry asked the angel, "At what point did Charles pray for me and Beatrice?"

The angel answered, "It was at the moment when you were having this particular argument and when you made this terrible comment. At that point Charles asked God for help. He may not have been able to explain all his feelings, but that is not important to God. It is not important to God whether you are intelligent, rich or a respected member of society. It is important that you have absolute trust and faith in God and ask for His help as a friend."

After a moment of silence the angel asked, "Do you have some American dollars in your pocket and do you have faith in the value of this currency?"

Harry was perplexed and said, "Why?"

"Just give me a bill and I will show you," answered the angel.

Harry took an American $20 bill out of his wallet and gave it to the angel. The angel took it and showed it to Harry.

"What do you see on the back side of this bill written like an emblem over the White House?" asked the angel.

Harry said, 'IN GOD WE TRUST'.

The angel said, "To my knowledge there is no other currency in this world issued by a government with the imprint 'IN GOD WE TRUST'. The American people, whether believers or non believers, as a community put their trust in God and express this trust also on their currency. I always wondered whether a true and convinced atheist would use an American dollar bill, being fully aware of the fact that this bill of exchange expresses trust not only in the value of the currency but also trust in God. Did you ever think about that?"

Harry said, "That thought never even occurred to me. But you are right, as a true and convinced atheist I should not handle that currency."

"On second thought," Harry continued with a smile, "my reason for being an atheist has changed since I met you. I am not concerned about using American dollars. The US dollar is one of the strongest currencies at present and I can surely see its value."

The angel said, "I knew you would come around to my way of thinking. But let's carry on with our train of thought. When you have trust in God, whom you may call your friend, what feelings will that create in you? Will you be happy? Will you be joyful or will you be scared of the responsibility you have to carry? You must realize that you will be consciously aware of the presence of God in your life. What kind of feeling will that create in you?"

Harry said, "That is a difficult question to answer. After all I am only one person among so many. I was never really consciously aware of the fact that the spirit of God lives in my soul. But if I have faith and trust in God's friendship then I can see myself being re-energized. I can see myself happy. I can see myself full of joy and hope. I can see myself as a lover who wants to spread this wonderful feeling of joy to all the others."

"Well spoken, my friend!" said the angel. "You see, I don't even need to call you a 'dried-up desert cactus' anymore. Instead I call you a friend who has the potential to move the mountains or blinders that block a clear vision of what is important and what is not important in your life."

"Harry," the angel continued, "we are almost at the end of our talk. We have covered the spirit of truth and love, faith in God's love, the desire to have life to the fullest in Heaven, the call to build God's kingdom and the joy of doing so. I would like to cover two more points that I consider important. I would like to discuss with you wisdom, the wisdom of God. God's wisdom, which has no deceit, will lead you to do what is right in the eyes of God. Would you mind if we discuss what is understood under God's wisdom?"

Harry said, "You know I was very skeptical in the beginning, but you were able to change my mind. I was shocked when you told me about the prayers of my son Charles. Now I feel very sorry that I ever made this comment."

He continued, "My friend, I hope I can call you a friend, I look forward to discussing wisdom with you. I am very sure that I will need all the wisdom in the world to make the right decisions when I go home and face my family. In fact, I will ask God to give me the wisdom of Solomon to find the right words when I talk to Charles and Beatrice."

The angel said, "You do not need the wisdom of Solomon. You need God's wisdom as help. I am sure that if you ask God, He will be very willing to help you. After all He is keenly interested in seeing that the prayers of Beatrice and Charles are answered."

THE WISDOM TO KNOW GOD'S WILL

THE ANGEL SAID, "WHEN YOU THINK of wisdom, you probably think of an old man, sitting in the silence in a forest alone by himself deep in thought. Am I right Harry?"

Harry nodded and said, "I guess so. I never really knew what wisdom is or how to describe it. I only know that when you make wise decisions, you will never be wrong. A wise man will always come up with a balanced view when making a decision, taking all the pros and cons into consideration. Am I right?"

"Just about!" answered the angel. "The only missing component of a wise decision is that the decision is inspired by God. God is the ultimate source of wisdom. In Him there is no deceit. In the Jewish scriptures wisdom is always compared to God's inspiration. You probably know that wisdom is feminine in most languages. It is the feminine side of God."

"If that is the case," said Harry impatiently, "then why are so many so-called wise decisions wrong?"

"In order to make a wise decision, you need time to think, time to pray, time to meditate. The power of meditation is enormous. In meditation you simply step back from your daily life and you take a rest."

The angel stopped for a moment. "You see the nature surrounding us here, the sun, the mountains, the ocean, all these invite us to meditation. It is wise to step back, enjoy and listen to God's word in your soul. God speaks quietly. God cannot be understood if you constantly surround yourself with a lot of noise, such as loud music or the rough and tumble of your business world. You need time for yourself to listen to God's word in your soul and to get to know His wisdom. His wisdom will guide you to do what is best for you."

Harry said, "You lost me! You tell me now that I should give up all the things I like to do and live like a hermit somewhere in the woods. If you ask me to give all these things up for the sake of wisdom and God's word in my heart, then I have to disappoint you. I am unwilling to do so because I enjoy the business life. By the way, I happen to be a realist. I have to live up to the demands of a certain lifestyle, which is expensive. I doubt that it would be wise to give up all these things which I enjoy."

"Don't get too upset with me!" said the angel with an ironic smile. "You don't have to give up very much. God would not dare to ask you for a great sacrifice. All I am trying to do is to make you aware that meditation has its great advantages, to set aside a moment for meditation and to ask what God wants from you is time never lost. It helps you to regain your strength and rejuvenates you. It also allows His word to take root in your soul."

Harry said, "You sure make me think. I was never really fond of meditation. I always was a man of action. But you are right. The many wrong decisions I made could have been avoided if I had only been a little bit more patient. I guess with meditation you get a more balanced view upon which you can make a wiser decision."

"Yes, you are right," said the angel. "I also still have to learn to be more patient, especially with a man whom I compared to a dried-up desert cactus. You see, even angels have room for improvements."

After a brief moment the angel continued, "Harry, I want to conclude our discussion. I was sent to answer the prayers of a child who deeply loves you. My mission is to help you to make a wise decision. I cannot make that decision for you. All I can do, is make you aware of God's will. I hope I gave you a glimpse of what is important in your life. God can be your best friend. God wants you to be guided to make the right decision and I was called to be your help. The choice is yours: See your tax accountants and lawyers, or go back to your family."

The angel continued, "I believe we are now at a point where we should take a moment of rest so that you can make a wise decision."

THE WISDOM TO DO GOD'S WILL

HARRY AND THE ANGEL SAT ON the bench quietly each occupied with their own thoughts. Harry suddenly was overcome by a wonderful feeling of love and warmth, a feeling that he had not experienced for many years. This warmth came from deep inside his body, like a new source of energy and power. It was a beautiful feeling of such indescribable tenderness. He felt the desire to hurry home and hug and kiss Beatrice and especially his son Charles.

Harry said to the angel, "I don't think that we have to discuss in great detail what God wants from me now. In this short moment of meditation, I suddenly realized my failings but also felt the enormous power of love. It is like a new source of energy coming from inside of my body. I suddenly feel free, the freedom of someone who had carried a great burden in his soul for a long time even though he didn't realize it. This burden is the wall I had built around me, which nobody was able to penetrate, not even Beatrice or Charles or my other children."

Harry continued, "I was so involved in my business affairs that I neither had the desire to communicate with my wife nor the desire to pay much attention to my children. I honestly believe now that I am the source of the unhappiness in my family. I always blamed it on everyone else. All of them tried to reach out to me, but I refused to let them come close to me. I never attempted a real communication, talking about what was really important, listening to what they had to say, touching them when a hug or handshake was needed, smiling when a smile of encouragement was required. I only was critical and cold."

Harry stopped for a while, but the angel encouraged him to carry on.

Harry said, "You know, I always blamed the lack of warmth and the lack of real communication on all the others, but not myself. How could they develop a real closeness to me when I rejected every approach? The wall that I believed Beatrice built around herself and Charles is really the reflection of the wall I had created in the first place. I was the one who started it first. I did not want anybody, especially any member of my family, to penetrate the security of this wall. I felt secure, but really I was not. I felt a sense of freedom within the borders of this wall, but this freedom was false. It was more an encampment and constraint than real freedom. I felt strong and invincible, but my strength was built on weakness. I thought I was happy but this happiness was the pretense that satisfaction comes from greed to achieve great wealth at all costs."

Harry stopped. The angel had listened patiently to Harry's confession. He realized that the first step to renewal was the acknowledgment of the wrongs done in the past.

The angel said to Harry, "What you said was beautiful. It was like the prayer you always wanted to say but never could express. Charles may be slow in learning and slow in school, but Charles has the capacity to express what is really important, namely absolute trust in God. He cannot express what is in his soul in words but he can express it with the look in his eyes. The burden that you so clearly identified in your confession will be lifted. You will be free; you will realize a new source of energy, an energy you never thought you had. You will love and you will be loved. That is the will of God. You may think that I, an angel sent by God, am a miracle. Let me tell you, there are angels in your daily life that are much closer to you than I ever will be. Maybe Beatrice is an angel; maybe Charles is one; maybe the people you meet are angels. You do not have to look far. How do you think I obtained this motorcycle?"

Harry said, "That is a question I have wanted to ask you. How did you do it and how did you learn how to drive it?"

"Well," said the angel, "God even has friends with the Hell's Angels. They sometimes don't realize that they can be real angels. The goodness in everyone comes from God, the goodness in caring for others, the goodness of making someone smile, all these things come from God. You just have to make the connection."

Harry said, "If there is hope for the Hell's Angels, then there is even hope for me, I guess."

"Of course there is," said the angel. "I have great hope and great faith in you, that you will make the decision that will result in real happiness and true freedom. I do not have to tell you what this decision should be. You will know it best yourself."

"Harry," the angel continued, "it is time that we say good-bye. You have work to do and so do I."

He continued with a shy smile in his eyes, "Can you help me with this machine? I am really not used to riding a motorbike. I still think I am driving a chariot."

Harry said, "No problem. That is the least I can do for you."

Harry and the angel picked up the motorcycle and Harry held it straight so that the angel could mount it easily. With great difficulty the angel started the engine, put it in first gear and drove toward the road north to Whistler. He waved with one of his hands and disappeared around the next corner.

HARRY AND BEATRICE, THEIR MARRIAGE RENEWED

THE SUN WAS STILL SHINING OVER the mountains to the west, lying low like a great orange ball.

Harry was still sitting on the bench deep in thought. Did he really meet an angel, or was it just a dream? He heard the traffic roaring by and reality sank in. He said to himself, 'I must have been crazy to think that an angel would visit me and talk about God and what is important in my life. Who am I to believe in such miracles? I am a man of reason who has no time for those esoteric spiritual thoughts of what is truth and what in life has real value. I am a businessman who must go on and create wealth and earn money for myself.'

Harry looked at his watch. 'You see,' he said to himself, 'it is still about 6 p.m. But why am I sitting on this bench? I was supposed to be driving to Whistler to meet with the tax lawyers.'

He suddenly remembered the reason for being there at the lookout. It was, of course, the blowout of his front tire. He remembered vividly the incident with that crazy motorcycle driver, the one he had almost killed. He remembered also that this man had stopped and introduced himself as an angel, not as a Hell's Angel but as a Heaven's Angel. So it must have been true that they had this talk, or was it? He recalled the many topics they had discussed, but he could not understand how it could still be about 6 p.m. Therefore, the discussion could not possibly have taken place. After all they must have talked for at least a few hours. He looked again in astonishment at his watch and recalled the comment the angel had made, that in eternity time does not exist. Did he really get a glimpse of eternity or was it just a hallucination? He could not come to a conclusion and decided to go back to his car and check the tire that had to be fixed.

There on the front tire imprinted just like the identification of the tire manufacturer were the following words: 'Do not be afraid, God loves you.' Harry looked again, and yes, these few words were clearly visible on the outside of the tire, not written with a crayon, but imprinted as a constant reminder. As long as he drove the car using this specific tire, Harry would be reminded of the dialogue that he had had with the angel.

Now a few of the points that they so intensely had discussed came back, culminating in the statement that it would be wise to do God's will, the will of a God who is at best described as a God of love whose spirit lives in all. All there was to do was to recognize this divine spirit and be more aware of its presence.

Harry felt suddenly the same warmth in his body that he had experienced when they had discussed the wisdom to recognize God's will. He remembered now the words an old professor from his days in the university had spoken. He had said, 'Love and do as you please. True freedom is to do the will of God'.

Harry opened the door to his car, started the engine and slowly moved to approach the road. He still was deep in thought and suddenly he remembered Beatrice and his son Charles. He recalled the wonderful days of his early marriage, the birth of the twins and also the birth of Charles. How could he resent Charles if even God would answer his prayers? How could he neglect Charles who had shown great love despite the fact that he, his father, had always thought him to be a nuisance? Even though he had been mistreated and mentally abused by his father, Charles had shown a great love for him.

Harry felt the same warmth that he had experienced when the angel was present. He said to himself 'I must go back to my family. I do love them all very much. I simply cannot destroy what is dear to me.' He wheeled the car around, screeching the tires. He thought that the angel would be relieved once he heard this screech as a sign that he was going back to where he belonged.

Impatiently, Harry raced the engine and the car sped toward Vancouver. At one of the exits, close to his home, he turned off the highway and stopped in a little flower shop. Initially he wanted to buy fifty red roses for Beatrice. Then he thought that it would seem to be like a fake. While in the flower shop the comment about a 'spiritually dried-up desert cactus' came to his mind. He said to himself: 'It would be a wonderful reminder of the talk I had with the angel, if I bought this cactus. Maybe Beatrice will not understand it, but I will. Whenever I build a wall around myself, whenever I am Harry the pompous fool, I will look at this cactus and say, 'Hey little plant, teach me a lesson!'

Harry purchased a small cactus with a few blue blossoms. He ran back to the car and was full of excitement as he approached his home. When he opened the door, he saw Beatrice with Charles sitting at the table both deeply involved solving some mathematical problems for school. Beatrice was as usual very patient while Charles tried diligently to write down some numbers in his schoolbook.

When Harry opened the door, they both looked up. They saw Harry excited like they had never seen him before. The dull and miserable expression on his face was gone. His eyes sparkled like they had never before. He took Beatrice's hand and pressed it to his heart. He also took the hand of Charles and cried out, "Beatrice and Charles get up fast! I want to hug and kiss both of you!"

The surprise in both of their eyes could not be overlooked. They had never seen this man so emotional and spontaneous. Every move or every word was always calculated and well-thought out. To their surprise, Harry was full of smiles and happiness.

He said to them both, "Beatrice and Charles I want to kiss and hug you. I want to start a new life. Yes, I was distant and cold, but I will change. Yes, I neglected you, my family, for all kinds of reasons, but I will change!"

"Beatrice, I love you very much!" he exclaimed. "I have not treated you very well in the past few months and our relationship was on the breaking point. My excuses were always reasons that were really not relevant. Beatrice, I want to change and I hope that you can forgive me. I really want you to be happy, as happy as we both were when we first started out in the adventure of our marriage. I want to do all the things we both promised ourselves we would do."

Beatrice could not believe her eyes and ears. Was Harry real? She had never seen Harry so full of excitement but when he took her in his arms, she felt the warmth of his body. Suddenly she also felt the same warmth coming from the depth of her body. She said, "Harry, I love you too. I have not said these words for so many weeks and months. They almost sound strange, but Harry, we both have to start again. Love is so wonderful. Many times I suffered, but I did not know why. I also was cold, had built a wall around myself not to be penetrated by anyone except our son Charles. He was my security for all these months and weeks when we could not find a common ground, when we could not jump over the walls we had built. Harry, let's not build these walls again."

Harry said with a smile, "Every time I become the pompous old Harry, look at this cactus I bought as a present. There is a story attached to this cactus, which I will tell you one of these days. Just have faith in my love for you and for all the children. Let us rejoice and be glad and celebrate."

Harry turned to Charles. Charles had watched in silence as his parents kissed and hugged, and he looked up with his deep, silent eyes. He said a prayer of thanks, not in words but in the expression of his face, a face that showed a deep understanding, deeper than his parents would ever realize.

Harry said to Charles, "Son, I am very proud of you. For me you are 'Charles the Great.' You are the one who brought me back to life and made me aware of what really is the 'ultimate' in this life. These are not things I treasured. The ultimate gift is love, the gift you share with both of your parents so freely. Just look at this little cactus I brought home. This cactus will blossom in the years to come and so will you. Your smiles will make people happy. I am glad you are my son and I am glad that you are alive and well."

Charles was speechless. He could not fully comprehend all the things his father had just told him, but he saw the blossoms on the little cactus and he smiled, a shy and innocent smile, but a smile full of love.

EPILOGUE

THERE WAS A CACTUS IN THE desert of Nevada. For years this cactus was dried-up and almost dead. Through a miracle this dried-up desert cactus started to bloom. It had magnificent blossoms. People would stop often when passing by and admire the beauty of this plant. Even the angel glanced at this cactus. While he admired the blossoms a smile brightened up his face and he said to himself. 'With a little bit of love and kindness everything that was dead can bloom again.'

RESEARCH SOURCES

THE NEW AMERICAN BIBLE: WASHINGTON, DC: United States Conference of Catholic Bishops, 2002. Print.

The Book of Genesis
The Book of Exodus
The Book of Wisdom
The Book of Daniel
The Gospel according to St. John
The Gospel according to St. Luke
The Gospel according to St. Matthew
The Letter of St Paul to the Hebrews
The Letters of St. Paul to the Corinthians
The First Letter of St. John
The Book of Revelations of St. John

Ianonne, John C. *The Mystery of the Shroud of Turin:* Staten Island, NY: Alba House,1998. Print.

Palmer, E.H. *The Koran – The Holy Book of Islam:* London, UK: Watkins Publishing, 2007. Print.

CPSIA information can be obtained
at www.ICGtesting.com
Printed in the USA
BVHW070643290122
627219BV00001B/78